BROKEN

Byrd Ranch Series - Book 1

JANA DAHMEN

Copyright © 2021 – Jana Dahmen
All cover art copyright © 2021 – Jana Dahmen
All Rights Reserved

This is a work of fiction. Names, places, characters and incidents are either the product of the author's imagination or are used fictitiously, and any resemblance to any actual persons, living or dead, businesses, organizations, events or locales is entirely coincidental.

No part of this book may be reproduced or transmitted in any form or by any means, electronic or mechanical, including photocopying, recording, or by any information storage and retrieval system, without permission in writing from the author.

Publishing Coordinator – Sharon Kizziah-Holmes
Cover Art – Jana Dahmen

Paperback-Press
an imprint of A & S Publishing
A & S Holmes, Inc.

ISBN -13: 978-1-951772-94-9

ACKNOWLEDGMENTS

Sharon Kizziah-Holmes at Paperback Press, **Shirley King McCann**, and **Kathleen Garnsey** are authors and friends whom I admire. I want to thank them for encouraging me along the way.

A thank you goes out to **Gary Schubert** in Sweetwater, Texas. He is a cowboy horse wrangler who is willing to share his knowledge of horses when I get it wrong!

I must thank my generous characters who are sharing their adventures with me. They live on the pages and between the lines. I can't wait to write the rest of their saga.

PROLOGUE

$\bullet \text{-} \{ \diamond \} \text{-} \bullet$

I n the darkness of night and the exhaustion of mind, body, and soul, Mary Ann no longer had a sense of direction. North, south, east, and west were all the same. She was lost, numbed from the cold, hungry, and hallucinating. Her mind played terrifying tricks distorting her reasoning. Pa, Comancheros, Comanches, and wild animals came at her from every direction. She couldn't separate the alarming visions from the miserable realities.

A thundering animal barreled out of nowhere and hit her horse from the side delivering a shocking blow. The trilling cry of an Indian pierced the wind at the same time. Sunny yipped and barked somewhere in the distance. Pegasus and another horse squalled and reared, pawing at the sky. The impact nearly knocked her out of the saddle. She lost the reins when she instinctively grabbed the pummel tightly with both hands and pulled against it to right herself with a surge of strength. She intuitively leaned her upper body low toward Pegasus's head until her cheek met his wet and lathered neck. Her heels dug into the stirrups to brace herself. She tightened her muscles in a spontaneous reaction.

Only by the skin of her teeth was she barely able to keep from sliding down Pegasus's back to the ground as his front hoofs reached high into the sky. It seemed like her horse stood straight up on his hind legs for a full minute. In truth, the whole episode happened so fast she didn't have time to consciously make decisions. For a girl who'd never ridden until getting to Byrd Ranch, managing to stay on Pegasus was an act of God. It was a wild trial by fire!

Without the reins she had no influence to keep Pegasus from a flat-out run to escape the melee. The marauding horse ran just as fast keeping up with the big white horse and eventually pulling ahead. Things couldn't get any worse until she realized an Indian now held her reins in one hand and was reaching out to grip the bridle with the other. Once Pegasus was slowed and brought under control, the Indian reached a sinewy arm out, snatching Mary Ann off and pulling her over to his horse. There was no saddle, and she scrambled to get fists full of the coarse mane, wrapping them around her hands. Mary was so overwhelmed; it hadn't even occurred to her she was once again captured.

Since Pa stole her away from Byrd Ranch, everything happening had been nightmarish. She fought hollering, kicking, hitting, twisting, grabbing, and yelling a string of profanities at the Indian she'd never used before. Then she cried and wailed. Nacona held on to her. He was surprised she was able to put up such an impressive fight. She made so much noise for a little one. He couldn't blame her for trying, but what did she think she could do against him? He held her close to his body until she drained herself near to collapsing. He spoke into her ear using a stern voice.

"Shut your mouth! Still yourself, and I'll let go of you."

"You'll let me go?"

"No! I'll let go of you, but I will not let you go."

He had her attention. She settled but then started sobbing uncontrollably. Again, he waited for the storm to roll over. Words would be wasted on a hysterical woman. She had a lot to cry out after all she'd been through. She had to know her pa was taking her to the flesh peddlers. Being handed over to such men would be a fate worse than death.

CHAPTER 1

---◆-◦❖◦-◆---

High Plains of Texas 1869

JD, Texas Marshall ◆

JD had been in a hard-ass saddle too many consecutive days. The young marshal from Spur, Texas was near the long journey's end. It had been an arduous week trailing the rustlers. He could feel every mile traveled and taste every stale biscuit and piece of jerky he'd eaten. The dust of the ground and the eye-watering stench of his own body motivated him to push through. He'd make it back home tonight if he had to ride in the dark.

The mere thought of all the hot water he wanted was luring him. The idea of toting and heating it himself didn't damper his enthusiasm. Damn, if he wasn't going to sleep clean and snuggly tonight on his own featherbed. The sparse room above the jailhouse was only big enough for a bed, dresser, and tub, but it provided him a place to clean up, let down, and sleep in private.

A man by himself didn't need many material things to hinder him. Just last year, he'd ridden into town on a horse with no name, his weapons, and a change of clothes. The powers in Austin had given him a badge, an assignment, a month's pay in advance, and sent him on his way to the office in Spur. JD was an official marshal for the state of Texas. The job carried a little clout but mostly heaping measures of headaches and responsibilities. He wouldn't have it any other way. The work could be dangerous but was satisfying.

On his first day in town, a herd of noisy school children spotted the shiny new star pinned to his vest. The prestige it represented drew them to him like bees to honey. He introduced himself as Marshal JD for the very first time. The young'uns responded excitedly, but what they most wanted to know was the name of his black horse. He'd answered, "No Name," but they'd misheard him to say, "New Man." He didn't bother to correct them as they repeated it over and over as children will do. So, his strong, black gelding with the constitution of iron became known as Newman from that time forward. It was the way of names and reputations. Good or bad, they tended to stick. Sometimes they just latched on and stayed where they landed with a grip not to be undone.

"Aw, hell!" JD spoke out loud.

He noticed something in the distance, and the discovery would make him get back later than he'd planned. A curled pillar of smoke rising in the northeast caught his attention. Expectations of a warm bath and a soft bed anywhere soon were put on hold. He wanted very much to ignore it, but he was duty-bound to investigate. A good marshal, and he was, could leave no stone unturned at the end of the day. The cause of so much smoke had to be determined. He was paid to keep an eye on Dickens County territory and all its people. This detour was inconvenient but unavoidable.

The plume looked to be nearabout Wicket, the ghost town about an hour's ride this side of Spur. He adjusted his direction accordingly to intersect with the fire within the hour. Most likely it would end up being nothing of consequence, but with the possibility of a prairie fire getting a toehold, he'd have to check it out. It was always better to be safe than sorry.

"Too bad Ole, Son," he spoke in a gentle voice to Newman. "This'll put us home after dark. Your extra oats will come late tonight."

JD was totally spent after riding with other lawmen for days to shut the rustlers down. The territory's ranchers were losing too much stock. He'd been called on to join a posse of guns to stop the hemorrhaging of beef. For him, the upside was riding with Ranger Grey Byrd again. They'd worked together several times and had become fast, dependable friends. In this hard country a good friend was more valuable than gold.

The two men had split up around midmorning to go their separate ways. Grey and his appaloosa stallion, Spanish Flight, angled off in the direction of Cap Rock in Garza County. JD had veered toward Spur. The two horses were bonded as well as their men and didn't much like parting. They were used to working together. The two horses were a natural team just like JD and Grey. It was for certain they'd be seeing each other again. There were always troubles to be sorted in this wild country.

Time spent along the Salt Fork of the Brazos River had been profitable. Catching the rustlers red-handed was a score for justice. Physical discomforts aside, it always felt good to make another win. Thank goodness no one in the posse had gotten hurt, but the thieves didn't fare so well. They were caught changing brands, and there was no question about what they were doing.

The rangers riding along had the authority from Austin to string rustlers up on the spot with no questions asked. Sadly, there were two young boys following their older brothers' examples. Texas deemed a cattle or horse thief guilty regardless of age. Old enough to steal was old enough to pay the price. JD and Grey hadn't stayed to witness them swing.

There were other rangers present who were less sympathetic and were more than happy to carry out the sentence.

Nearing the deserted settlement brought JD to the source of the fire. It was the legendary haunted cabin partially standing and still smoldering. What a fitting end to a house so burdened by past tragedy. A whole family had been found murdered in here many years ago. A pioneer sodbuster had built the place for his bride and never dreamed his family would die from gunshot wounds while lying in their beds. This was called the house of death for a reason.

The who and why of the killings remained a mystery. The story was ripe fodder for ghost stories, and the tales grew completely out of proportion over the years. The deathly quiet place became quite an infamous landmark over time.

Young men capitalized on the ghost lore by bringing their girls here hoping they'd be frightened enough to seek their manly comforts. Then they'd collect rewards for saving them in the form of kisses. The site was well-visited even though it was all a big ruse. Now, the old icon was mostly gone.

He was tempted to just ride on past. The fire had burned down with no danger of spreading. A few bright embers still glowed, the smoke was waning, and the wind had settled. He was curious though and rode a slow circle around what was left.

The front of the structure had caved in hiding the interior. In the back, a splintered door was still hanging open by a cracked leather hinge. JD left Newman ground tied and upwind from the smoke, He wet his bandana with canteen water, then wrapped it over his mouth and nose as a filter against the caustic smoke. He wrenched what was left of the hot, door loose and got a darkened glimpse of the inside.

"Oh, my Lord!" JD breathed with only himself and God to hear.

Unmistakably, he could make out the form of a body lying under a tangle of collapsed debris. He couldn't see much detail, but a tabletop had fallen and was partially covering the person. Without hesitating, he rushed in with little expectation anyone could have survived the inhalation of smoke.

Damn, it's a girl!

He was not expecting to find anyone in the first place, and then for it to be a girl was harder to fathom! It was a damn shame in a country where females were so scarce. By a miracle, she'd been shielded somewhat from the heat and cinders. The table had insulated her from the harshest of the flames, but he had to assume she was dead. The smoke and lack of fresh air had most likely been suffocating. He checked quickly for a pulse anyway. He let out a shout of triumph as he felt the faintest beat of life. Throwing her over his shoulder, he bolted into the fresh air clearing the three rickety steps outside the doorway in one leap.

He ripped the bandana off his face and gulped in the fresh air. Then he laid her on the soft, cool prairie grass in the fading light of pending dusk. The marshal settled her onto one side to avoid the burns, blisters, and trauma apparent on her back. He searched her bruised and battered face to see if he recognized this girl. The large knot above her eyebrow made him cringe.

"Mary Barton!" he exclaimed out loud to no one.

He'd only caught glimpses of her from a distance in town, so JD couldn't be completely positive this was Mary Barton. If he had to guess now, he'd say it was. Much to his shame he'd never checked on her welfare. Mary was BB Barton's daughter, and nobody liked him. Shamefully, she was overlooked by association with the town drunk. The schoolboard hired her, on the schoolteacher's insistence, to clean the schoolhouse, stack the wood, stoke the wood stove, and do other odd jobs. She did the work at night. Afterward she picked discarded items she could use or leftover food from trash piles around the town. No one complained, so he'd left her alone.

How in the hell did she end up here in this condition? Who brought her out this far from Spur? It seemed too far for her to have walked. If this was indeed the Barton girl, BB had serious questions to answer.

How did you get here?

Her sooty clothing was in bad repair. From the looks of it, the tearing and injuries were made before the fire started. Welts indicated she'd been beaten. Bruises on her arms indicated rough handling. The bump on her head looked angry. She was filthy, her body was indecently covered. It didn't take a lawman to put two and two together. Mary Barton had been physically attacked, but by whom?

On a quick, chaste assessment of bruising and signs of blood, there was no doubt she'd been breached. Old marks on her body spoke of her pa's past harsh treatment. All the pain and neglect this girl had obviously endured during her life made him sick to his stomach. JD would make anyone responsible for hurting her regret it.

What kind of monster treated you this badly?

No way was the fire accidental. The flames were set to destroy the crime. Without further delay, he had to get her to the doctor in town as soon as possible. It was all up to him and Newman to get her there. The whole of this story could be dealt with later. The doctor might be able to fill in more pieces of what happened to her.

He whistled, and the horse ran to him straightaway. The dirty, smelly blanket from his bedroll would have to serve as a wrap. It had been a week on the trail and tied to the back of his horse, but it couldn't be helped. Carefully moving her, he pulled the sides up loosely covering her bruised and exposed body. Her breaths came in shallow, short, labored rattles emphasizing the physical stress she was under. The dark swelling on her head kept worrying JD. Every minute he could keep her breathing provided hope. He moistened her lips from his canteen but attempts to give her drips of water caused strangling. He abandoned the effort.

Not knowing if she would make it to town alive, he lay her across his saddle and mounted behind her. Doing his best not to injure her further, he gently pulled her onto his lap and cradled her to his body with one arm. It was the best he could do. A few barely audible groans protested the movements, and JD chose to interpret the moans as good signs. Pushing Newman as hard as he dared in the dark, he offered up a prayer, and rode toward help.

CHAPTER 2

Ranger Greyson Byrd ✦

R anger Grey Byrd never dreamed every normal and
routine circumstance of his life would be in complete
shambles only four months after riding out with JD
and the posse to catch the rustlers. Everything he'd counted
on as being forever was turned upside down and inside out
now. Pain, remorse, what-ifs, absolute fear, and one tiny
baby girl running out of time held his mind a prisoner and
paralyzed him in place.

One of Grey's many strengths was being a logical and
methodical thinker under pressure. Being able to figure out
what to do in bad situations made him an excellent ranger.
Today, he'd lost his edge and found himself backed into a
corner with no plan whatsoever. He was totally broken by
his wife's sudden, traumatic death. On top of losing Beth, he
didn't know how to save their baby, little Sari, his own flesh
and blood.

Kneeling beside Beth's freshly laid grave, Grey was a
terrified man. He didn't even recognize himself. Factors he
thought were important had become non-priorities. Grief had

his senses firing in unfamiliar ways, and he was having trouble organizing his thoughts. He mindlessly rubbed, smoothed, and worried the rough mound of red, clay clods covering his wife. He worked from one end of her grave to the other and then started the process over. The work of his calloused hands served no purpose, but he couldn't make himself stop.

He fisted hard chunks of clay and could feel the warmth from the hot afternoon sun. It brought him no measure of relief. Six feet under, right where he kneeled, lay the cold, silent body of his good wife, Sari's mother. He understood she'd moved beyond the confines of this earth the moment she breathed her last breath, but the undeniable, irrational urge to dig Beth up was intense. This had to be a mistake or a nightmare, didn't it? No, what was done was irreversible, and he had to find a way to deal with it.

Tears mixed with the reddish dirt collected in his moustache and streaked his face. Along with his growth of short whiskers, he looked no better than the scruffy outlaws he pursued. This demonstrative, emotional breakdown had been coming for the last two days. He'd held off giving into his weakness until well-meaning friends and neighbors left the ranch. Most of all, he'd needed his wife's meddling cousin to get away and out of his sight. He didn't want to ever lay eyes on the woman again, but he knew Wisteria would be back. She always came back.

With no audience or reason to hide his anguish any longer, the dam he'd built cracked and split apart. Sorrow poured directly from the deep well of his heart. Freely, swell after swell of audible sadness rolled out of him as surges of wet tears fell like rain. Disappointment at the loss of how things were supposed to be tore through him like a stampede of wild Mustangs. He'd never experienced such a trampled and crushed spirit before this day. The uncertainties of what was to come blurred his dreams. Each fresh onslaught of sorrow weakened him physically and left him trembling. It also shored up his determination to save their little baby girl at all costs.

Beth's death was tangible, and no amount of weeping changed or made things easier. God didn't allow the dead to come back to earth for a reason. The body of his loving, loyal wife and Sari's mother lay at rest forever. Her shell was buried beneath his hands, but her soul had been released to soar. She no longer had a voice to tell him out loud how to proceed, but he had no doubt she could speak to his heart.

Grey threw his head back as he stood, spreading his arms wide open to the big sky. He looked to the heavens for divine help knowing with his heart and soul God would not leave him defenseless. He asked Him for good judgment and doable solutions. He listened hard and patiently, but nothing sounded immediately in answer to his prayers.

Even though he felt without direction like a lone, untethered tumble weed rolling and bumping across the prairie, Grey did not lose faith. The ball of his emotions traveled this way and the other not making progress or reaching anywhere. Grey shuddered and doubted he could do this alone, but he knew Jesus would point the way.

"Which direction am I to go? Give me some options, please. What is Your plan? I can't do this without Beth!" He listened as hard as he could, and yet no answers came.

Pulling a faded bandana from his back pocket, he wiped with disappointment at the dirt and tears. He'd never been the type of man who spilled tears, but at this moment, he finally understood what could lead a man to it. He'd been so shortsighted. Guns and a badge hadn't protected Beth, nor could they be of any use in saving Sari. In only a moment, everything important to him started failing and falling. Grey's perspective on life changed in a moment. He'd been brought to his knees, helpless, when those he loved came under attack.

I may well be down, God, but I'm not giving up on You. Please, show me how to fix this.

It was time to cowboy-up! Upstairs, lying on the thin precipice between life and death, his daughter was depending on him. He'd do anything, no matter the cost, to rescue her. He blew his nose, pushed his hat down firmly on his head, and squared his broad shoulders preparing for the fight.

Two days ago, he'd made a promise to God he'd never run from his responsibilities to family and home again. He'd give up being the kind of man his people couldn't count on for protection.

Beth, I won't abandon our girl regardless of what it takes.

"Make me aware of what to do next. I mean dang it, Beth. I wasn't supposed to be doing this alone! Our little birdy is so fragile. Doc is trying everything he can think of to get her fed. Nothing stays down, because she needs your milk. Every passing minute comes closer to being Sari's last.

"Send me a sign, Darlin'. Give me any action to take; any direction to go. Please, I'll do it, no matter what. I want our child to live! I want a second chance to do something right."

Doc ◆

Doc was out of breath from the effort of climbing to the top of the hill to get a word with his friend. Grey was standing alone by Beth's grave in the family cemetery and staring off into the distance. It was inconsiderate to intrude on a man in mourning, but he had to talk to him immediately.

"Belle said I'd find you here. I apologize, but we must talk. What I have to say won't keep."

Grey cleared his throat and made his voice sound as steady as possible.

"Sure, Doc, let's get to it. My time is all about Sari now. I have a lifetime ahead to grieve, but the baby may only have a short time. If anything can be done, I mean anything, I swear I'm gonna do it!"

"A wet nurse cannot be found. I've followed up on every

lead in this territory to no avail. No one is available or feeling in a position to help. The closest possibility I found is a whore who dropped a stillborn. I examined her. The woman has advanced consumption, and the illness makes her unsuitable. She's in a sad situation of her own.

"We'll keep asking God for His help. We won't give up, but if something doesn't change, and soon, you must prepare yourself for the worst. Sand keeps trickling through the hourglass and there are only so many grains left.

"I'm starting a new treatment. It's a Comanche trick I've only heard about. I know it's no fix but might buy us some extra time for two or three days at the most.

"I told Smith to kill your youngest, healthiest calf and cut its liver out. He's doing it now. I instructed Belle to boil the liver in water, then strain the broth through a cloth at least three times. If Belle can coax Sari to keep drops of this rich liquid down, it may provide the nutrients she's needing for a short while.

"There's something else for you to consider. It's not near as easy as killing a calf, I'm afraid. It might be the only solution though, so hear me out. What I'm suggesting is complicated. You're at the end of the rope. I fear this is the last knot left for you to grab.

"A young woman living in Spur is of sound health, except she's been recovering from an attack. One of the trespasses against her resulted in a pregnancy. She's right at four months along with no one to marry her, no money, and no home. There is no family to help her or the baby. The girl is quite alone and destitute.

"She does have a pa, the town drunk. He's not worth his skin and not to be trusted. The marshal can't even find him. He caused all the trouble by putting his own girl up as stake in a card game. He lost. She had to ante up. You can guess what it took for her to settle the debt. In addition, she was badly hurt and almost died after she was left in a burning house.

"The marshal found her barely alive and got her to the doctor. Miraculously, she survived. Her pa conveniently disappeared, just vanished. The marshal's trying to locate him with no luck so far. The three men who hurt her got clean away.

"An old neighbor lady, the girl has been kind to over the years, returned the favor. She gave her room and board in exchange for chores, but her nephew just sold the little homestead. He'll be taking his aunt to live with relatives in Arkansas, and the girl must vacate the place. She's stranded with nothing. She has no friends except for the doctor and marshal. They like her a lot and speak quite highly of her, in fact.

"No one else in the community has or will raise a hand to help her. It's just, well, you know people, Grey. They only see she's pregnant out of wedlock, and they despise her pa. Whether the girl is a victim or not makes no difference to them. She's a ruined woman in Spur. She, or the baby, will ever be welcomed there."

"That's a long, pitiful story. Why are you tellin' me all this, Doc?"

"I wanted you to have all the details because this young woman can give Sari the milk she needs. I can't advise you what to do, Grey, but maybe you should think about going to get her. She's the only one who can help Sari. If it's possible to save your baby, you need this girl.

"Grey, you and I both know how hard a place West Texas is to survive. We've heard the stories of men marrying out of necessity. A few with children to care for have even had to remarry on the very day their wives have died. A man will do almost anything for his children.

"This girl I speak of needs a husband, and Sari deserves a fighting chance. You have little time to ponder this before you make the decision. This young woman needs you as much as you need her. She could take care of your baby now, and you could take care of hers when it's born. If you claim her, you'll both have a fair chance of putting the shattered pieces of your lives back together. Good marriages have been built on less.

"She can give Sari what you cannot. She will be able to provide milk right away with proper nutrition, care and being exposed to the baby's cries and suckling. It will be enough to cause her milk to drop since nature is already preparing her body to support her own baby."

With nothing more to add, Doc turned on his heels and started down the hill.

Greyson whispered for only God to hear.

"Thank You, Lord. You didn't wait long to point the direction. My answer is a yes. I'm going to obey You and go immediately. I understand and will do what I must. Beth and I both thank You. Sari means everything to us.

"Beth you were the best wife any man could have. I love you Beth, and I love Sari. Going after this girl means no disrespect to your memory, Darlin'. Our baby is my priority now. Go with me to Spur. Help me say the right words to persuade a scared girl to trust me with her life."

CHAPTER 3

———•◆◦✦◦◆•———

Cousin Wisteria Winters ✦

Wisteria Winters was fit to be tied and struggling to contain her temper. Attending Cousin Beth's long-winded funeral was absolutely the most wearisome place she'd ever been trapped. Beth had never been anything but a trial to her over the years and standing here for all this dribble was another test of patience. She wanted to scream, "Enough already!" If the appalling woman wasn't dead, she'd take great pleasure in killing her all over again.

Belle, Beth's tedious sister-in-law, had already overstepped her bounds this morning. She'd humiliated her publicly by assigning Wisteria to stand with the general crowd of onlookers. She'd boldly declared it loudly enough for others to overhear. Wisteria had to hold her hand down to keep from slapping the smug look off Belle's face.

"Only the very immediate family will be seated in chairs at the front. Everyone else will stand behind them," she'd said.

How dare she humiliate her so publicly by erasing her

from the family tree. There was nothing to do about the barefaced snub without creating a costly scene. Wisteria would not be coerced into showing her hand just yet. She'd have to wait for a while longer until her plans were well underway to minimize resistance. The Byrds wouldn't know what hit them.

Only four chairs from the house had been carried up the hill in honor of the small family. Smith and Coley, Grey's brothers, had taken their seats. and Belle sat in the chair between her husband and Grey. Belle was the loose woman Smith had rescued from a local saloon and then married. It was a slap in Wisteria's face this whore garnered more respect than she did.

From the very moment Smith brought her here she had caused Wisteria nothing but annoyances. She was too smart and nosey for her own good. The bitch was bright, street smart, and questioned every decision Wisteria made. She was constantly sneaking around observing anything and everything having to do with Beth's care. In the most subtle of ways the girl meddled in Wisteria's affairs. No one ever noticed the steam building between them. This past year Wisteria had been on guard and meticulously careful about covering her tracks.

Once, when Belle became sick after eating leftovers from Beth's luncheon tray, Wisteria was afraid she'd been exposed. Only a low bred commoner eats from someone else's plate. Luckily, Belle's discomfort was explained away as indigestion from a stomach ailment. Since then, the animosity between them had only escalated.

Soon, very soon, Wisteria would marry Grey and take over as the new mistress of Byrd Ranch. There were many axes to grind, and Belle would be the first who'd feel the torturous cut of a dull blade. Her fate was sealed, and Wisteria looked forward to making her suffer. One more murder added to her lengthy list was nothing. Killing was a rewarding game, and she was a psychopath with refined skills.

She did have to admit she'd botched Beth's murder. Things had not gone as planned. At this very moment, her tiny baby girl lay dying a slow death from the effects of the Prussic acid she'd spoon fed her mother. She was only alive due to Belle's stubborn ministrations. Her attention to the spawn was delaying the inescapable. The infant was wasting away from the residual effects of the poison passed onto her from her mama. Dammit, hadn't she slipped the woman ample amounts to kill them both in one fell swoop? Apparently, she had not.

No one was going to stand between Grey and herself ever again, especially this baby. Grey was as good as in her bed already. This long, tiring game of cat and mouse was finally coming to an end. Wisteria had only allowed time to drag by this long because she'd learned so much about herbs and poisons by using Beth as a living guinea pig. As soon as the dust settled from burying both mother and baby, she'd sprint to the goal line.

Wisteria wanted to slip away and smother the child to death right now. She couldn't because someone was stationed in the nursery with her. Otherwise, it would be so quick and easy to move forward. Everyone knew the infant was as good as gone already, and her demise would never be questioned.

Really, this untidy setback was just as much Doc's fault. If he hadn't fought so heroically to save the newborn, it would be lying in the stiffened arms of its mother's cold corpse at this very moment. All evidence of a crime ready to be lowered on ropes and buried six feet under in one comfy coffin forever. It would save the trouble of digging a second hole! The mere thought of enduring a second funeral for the baby was ridiculous. Wisteria could never catch a break!

The harsh climate of West Texas was not kind to fragile ladies. It was no wonder there were so few gentle women to be counted in this dreary land. The black net of the mourning veil offered little protection for Wisteria's face in the onslaught of the constant wind. To make it worse the gale was hot, dry, and loaded with sand brushing across her paper-thin skin like a carpenter's sandpaper. The exquisite complexion she so painstakingly tended was going to be reddened and chapped by the time she got back to the house. The damage would take weeks to repair with applications of restorative herbs and creams.

Rogue gusts whipped the long skirts around her legs making them snap like a flag. It was tearing at her hair causing wisps to fall from her carefully piled and pinned coiffure. Vanity kept her from exposing herself to the raw elements, but there was no way she could have refused to come. The hungry gossipers would love the fodder of her absence.

There was no shade to block the burning rays of the sun. The pungent odor of fresh manure made the eyes water. This misery was teetering on the brink of being too much to bear. West Texas was best suited for insects, crawling creatures, cowboys, and simple, farm women.

The one saving grace was having the chance to steal glances at handsome Grey. He was a man with a strong, tall stature and wide shoulders giving him a brawny appearance. He was delicious like candy to Wisteria's eyes. What an imposing figure he cut! Beth's ranger had always been the one she wanted, and now, he was all hers. They could finally be together.

She tapped the toe of one well-heeled boot in a steady rhythm. Her limbs were quivering with fatigue as she baked in the blasted oven of the outdoors. Perspiration ran down her back. The parson droned on in monotone extolling Beth's perfect attributes. He listed her many contributions to the community. He read the scriptures defining a good wife and her value to her husband and in the eyes of the Lord. Beth was a saint, would be missed, and blah, blah, blah!

The only way she made it the last few minutes came in

the form of an unrelenting horsefly. It buzzed loudly, dodging in and out of the crowd, landing on one and then another. It was swatted away to make the rounds in and out of the crowd. It was a persistent devil.

As the preacher was beginning to wind down, a child screeched and squalled out in pain. The blood sucker had finally gotten his pound of flesh! The boy's father slapped to kill hitting his son hard enough to make him howl even louder than he was already crying. The commotion was a fitting climax to the dull hour squandered in the wind.

Wisteria was a serial killer. She craved the heady feeling of power it gave her over people and became addicted to it. Her first kill had been her own mother, Roxanna. Wisteria was fascinated to find how easy it was to commit murder without raising suspicion. Her mother could attest to this if she wasn't long dead, buried, and eaten by worms. The whole town of Caprock had been shocked to learn of Roxanna Winters' untimely death, but no one ever questioned the cause.

Their friend had been at church on a Sunday morning complaining of slight indigestion. By Wednesday morning she couldn't be revived after a wicked bout of dysentery. The doctor pronounced her dead of natural causes. She was laid to rest on Thursday at sunrise. On the following Sunday, Wisteria, attended church alone. It had gone just that quickly. Since then, Wisteria had learned so much more about the mystery of herbs. Prussic Acid was nice addition to her arsenal, along with arsenic, and various pest poisons used in homes.

Wisteria never liked her mother. She rarely thought of her anymore except to recall the fun of watching the surprise on her mother's face when it dawned on her Wisteria was the one making her sick. By then, it was too late. The point of no return had been reached, and the damage was irreversible. Wisteria had laughed at her ignorance and agony until her dying breath.

Teas and foods laced with lethal quantities of herbs detrimental to the digestive system were simple to introduce in Roxanna's diet. She was none the wiser. Wisteria had even ground something into her mother's tooth powder. It was an ingenious and creative trick! There was no need to kill the woman slowly since they lived alone together in the same house. No one was watching. It was a lucky touch Roxanna complained of feeling poorly at church for all her friends to hear. It laid the groundwork for the news of her death.

There was not the slightest inkling Roxanna had been poisoned by her only and loving child. No one even knew Wisteria had an interest in herbs and had been dabbling in them for quite some time. For effect, Wisteria mourned demonstrably in her mother's honor and remembrance at the gravesite. Wisteria pulled off the perfect crime and the success whet her appetite for studying, learning more, and practicing her new favorite craft. It was amazing how gullible and trusting people could be. Wisteria marveled at the ability to murder someone right under their noses.

As an only child, Wisteria inherited everything which included the house, belongings, and monies. She'd long coveted the financial inheritance she was entitled to receive. She perfected her business skills by investing and cheating shrewdly. She became an independent woman of wealth overnight. Keeping sharp eyes and ears open, she stayed on top of the opportunities and could spot a fool a mile away. Through manipulations and crooked practices, her holdings multiplied seven-fold. She had no scruples and no qualms about dealing under the table.

Beth had been a festering thorn in her side her entire life. Wisteria's whole world revolved around coveting whatever her lucky cousin possessed whether it was real or abstract. Jealousy is very much the green-eyed-monster, and she made it hard on an unsuspecting Beth at every turn. In Wisteria's warped and selfish mind, Roxanna preferred Beth over her in every way. Wisteria thought she saw and heard her cousin being heaped with praises, adorations, and good things. All the while, in her thinking, she was thrown the scraps. Hate made her greedy and mean-spirited. She could never steal enough of what belonged to her cousin.

CHAPTER 4

————— ♦ ❖ ♦ —————

Mary Ann Barton ♦

Mary Ann had a sinking, nauseous feeling in the pit of her stomach as she watched the buckboard disappear out of sight. She continued to stare down the road long after it was gone. Living with the old woman had been a safe place to recuperate and gain some strength. She received her room and board in return for light work. The old woman gave her a kindness she'd never had before.

She'd understood the arrangement was temporary from the beginning, but if only it could have lasted through the winter. The grandson came this morning to take his grandmother away to live with family in Arkansas. He'd put the little homestead up for sale, and it sold quickly. Mary Ann knew of no place to go where she'd be safe. She'd always had to take care of herself, but now, there was the baby to consider. She was familiar with being alone, but she was not familiar with feeling frightened to be alone. This was a new fear, and it made her sad.

The shack where she'd lived with Pa was still standing

empty and in the same poor condition it had always been. It offered a leaky roof, hard work, hunger, and the possibility Pa might return any day. Never would she go back there to live under him. If he came back, she might not be able to get away from him again. She would not expose her baby to live under his cruelty.

Memories of what happened four months ago were fuzzy and only came back to her in unexpected fragments. She couldn't grasp the flashes long enough to examine them. The one thing she did remember clearly was Pa dropping her off and leaving her in the hands of danger. Not only had he given her away, but he'd almost gotten her killed in the fire.

A chilling shutter ran through her as she had a fleeting image of a horrible man looking at her with one eye, but then he was gone. Mary Ann was thankful she couldn't remember details. Whatever happened to her must have been awful. Pa was mean and selfish, but he'd never handed her over to someone before. He'd beaten her. He'd not replaced the milk cow when it died or gotten more chickens when they played out. They were her main sources of food, but he didn't eat at home. What she ate or didn't eat was of no concern to him. She never remembered not being hungry.

She'd taught herself to hunt small game with a slingshot she'd found and by setting crude traps. She'd foraged constantly, digging in the dirt for roots and grubs, and picked through trash piles in town. She took any useful leavings such as worn-out clothing, things she could read, and table scraps.

What a blessing the schoolboard had agreed to hire her to help the teacher with chores. The only stipulation was she stay out of sight. She'd been paid a small sum, but it was enough for a little sugar, flour, cornmeal and such for one person. The teacher taught her to read, write and do numbers, and gave her access to books. Mary Ann had a thirst for knowledge and quickly learned to teach herself. Books and papers opened the world to her.

Pa disappeared for days at a time, and she liked it better when he was gone. Mary Ann never asked where he went and had no desire to know. He may have worked somewhere but didn't spend any earnings on her if he did. No doubt he drank and gambled his money away. She disliked him, but not near as much as he despised her.

When she was well enough, the marshal questioned her about how she ended up in the burning house. Marshal JD was disappointed she couldn't tell him much. He had a few facts he shared with her. He said Pa had bet her in a card game to some bad men. He lost the hand, she got hurt, and they all disappeared. She wasn't surprised, but the truth was hard to hear. If she ever saw Pa again, she'd thank him for giving her the courage to leave his house. The degrading insults and pain she'd suffered under the hands of BB Barton were now in the past.

The marshal said he'd found her barely alive in the fire. The agony of healing made her wish he'd left her there to die. The misery the doctor put her through was worse than the injuries. Weeks later, when he noticed she was carrying a child, her attitude changed. The news gave her a reason to live. She'd never considered having a child of her own. A tiny person, a sweet, innocent life was growing inside of her. It was dependent on her for protection, she took the responsibility seriously.

Mary Ann didn't have a clue what happiness looked like, but she was determined to keep her eyes open for it and make the best choices she could. She decided her baby would be happy. Foremost on her list was to find a safe, warm place to winter. Out of habit, her arms and hands reached around cradling the small, bulge of her belly. Useless tears rolled down her sallow cheeks. Tears disgusted her anytime she gave into the weakness of crying. The salty brine from tears ran down her face and found the seam between her lips. It ran across the path with the taste of despair.

What an exposed state to find herself. A disgraced girl

and a baby with no father's name were vulnerable. What chance in this world did they have without a man's name to shield them? She felt the welfare of this child weighing on her small shoulders, and the weight was crushing her.

"Baby I have nothing to give to you but my love, not even a home or a warm winter's fire, but don't you worry little one. I believe God will make a way for us," she whispered. "I may not remember the day you were made, but the angels who were in attendance know it all. They're still watching over us. I pray this is so."

Mary Ann had faith, and she refused to accept defeat. Wallowing in self-pity was a destructive option, but right now exhaustion engulfed her without warning, and she wasn't thinking straight. Suddenly, she felt weak, shaky, and tired to the bone. It was all she could do to get back to the house. She'd nap on her pallet and then figure out what to do later. Little did she know a ranger by the name of Greyson Byrd would soon be on his way to rescue her and the baby.

Greyson Byrd ✦

The girl Doc spoke of was in the next county, and Grey was leaving to locate her as soon as humanly possible. Beside the gravesite, while Doc was still talking, he'd made up his mind. She held the key to Sari's life in her hands, and he was hell bent on bringing her back here to Byrd Ranch. He saddled the big white horse in haste. He was the strongest and most dependable mount on the ranch, and the stallion had the grit for hours of hard riding. He was built for endurance and could easily carry two riders for long distances through scrub country.

He was the horse Beth chose to ride, and somehow it made him feel like she was going along. She'd named the ole son, Falling Snow. They had an arduous journey ahead in the dark. The sun would be setting soon, but Grey refused to wait until daybreak.

There was no time to waste, Grey pushed ahead only stopping to rest the horse when it was the right thing to do. The clock in his head was ticking with the beat of his heart. Precious seconds were being marked off with a loud, steady rhythm. Belle had hurriedly packed his saddle bags with more than enough provisions for two, and Smith tied a bag of oats to the back of his saddle. His family was optimistic he'd find this young woman suitable and willing.

With Belle's typical boldness, she sent him off with a challenge. "Do not come back without her."

CHAPTER 5

---◆◇◈◇◆---

Greyson Byrd ◆

The shadow of a familiar landmark revealed Grey had just crossed over into Dickens County. He would be on the outskirts of Spur within the hour. There would be time to spare before sunup. Man, and horse could eat and rest before coming face to face with the one he'd come to claim. JD would have information on the girl he was looking to find.

The first stop was the livery stable. Snow had earned a break before heading out again tomorrow. He tossed the night hostler an extra coin for rousing him from his cot. He asked the sleepy-headed boy to take extra good care of his tired horse. The ranger's badge Grey wore garnered a large degree of respect. Hero worship ensured the youth would do his best.

From there he walked to the darkened jail to stir JD from his warm bed. The two lawmen had been acquainted for a long time and their bond was cemented in trust. His living quarters were above the jail, and Grey gave a holler before climbing the stairs to the outside entrance. It wasn't wise to surprise a man who kept a loaded gun close at hand. Grey felt a sudden yearning to unburden his woes to his friend. He could tell JD what was in his heart about Beth and the fear of losing their baby. It all lay heavily on his mind, and he needed to vent to the best friend he had besides Smith and Coley.

JD stoked the embers in the office woodstove and put on a fresh pot of coffee for them. From a cupboard he pulled down a battered tin of fresh bread, butter, and a jar of preserves. Soon the soothing aroma of coffee and scrambled eggs filled the air around them. The two settled down to break bread and talk. JD sensed Grey's heaviness, and he listened without interruption while his friend recounted the nightmare he'd been living for the past few days.

"Amigo, I have no idea what to say to you." JD sympathized shaking his head. "I heard about Beth's sudden passing, and I knew you were taking a hard hit. I'm glad you feel comfortable to entrust me with your heartache. How can I help you, Ole Son? I'm glad to listen and ready to do anything to be of help. I'm here for you and ready. You just say the word. I can only imagine how torn up your heart is right now."

Looking sorrowfully at his friend for a moment, he added, "I know Beth was a good woman, the best woman. I never met a finer one, in fact. I'm so regretful, Grey, you've lost your special person. Everyone she touched was blessed some way or the other. She always made me feel welcome to sit at your table."

"It's true, JD, Beth looked after everybody around her. She was totally selfless. I didn't realize just how completely I loved her and depended on her until it was too late to do better. Now I feel the guilt of being gone from home so much and for not telling her regularly how much I loved her. I could have done more to make her life better."

"How you must be worrying about your baby girl! Doc can't do anything for her?"

"No medicine is going to fix Sari. Doc and Belle have been working together around the clock without making headway. They were starting something new as I rode out. Even if it works, it's not a long-term solution. It will just buy a little extra time. I can't lose her, JD. I just can't. It's why I've ridden the night to get here."

"Okay, explain, so I can understand."

"I came because I'm looking for someone. There's a girl here your doctor has been treating, but I don't even know her name, JD. Doc said she's gonna have a baby and has no husband. The second I heard about her situation, I headed here to convince her to go home with me. You know of this girl, right?"

"I do know the girl very well, in fact." JD nodded his head slowly but made no other comments. There was silence between the men for a moment.

"I have to hear everything you know about her. I have to find her soon before it's too late for Sari."

The marshal looked at him showing no discernable expression on his face and still said nothing. JD's cocked eyebrow made Grey realize he wasn't making much sense. He had to slow down, pull it together and make his thoughts clearer. He had to communicate precisely why he was here at this odd hour and exactly what he expected. He had to make JD understand the urgency of the situation with the rest of the story.

"Doc can't locate a wet nurse for Sari, but this girl's misfortune could be our saving grace. He says she can produce the milk Sari needs, right away, even before her own baby is born. I'm going to plead with her to go back with me to Byrd Ranch as soon as possible. She's the one who can feed Sari. She's the one person who can save her life."

Almost out of breath, Grey added, "Please, tell me anything and everything you know about the girl I've come to fetch. Also, I need to know where to find her."

JD stood up and walked around the room, collecting his

thoughts for a moment, before he spoke. "The girl you're looking for is Mary Ann Barton. She's an extraordinary individual. What you've come to ask of her, well, it's a lot after what she's already been through. I can see how it might be in her best interest to comply. I can hear in your voice how frantic you are for her help, Grey, but I don't want Mary to feel bullied into something she doesn't feel comfortable doing. She'll go with you only if she desires to help. She's a good, kind, smart girl with a pure heart of gold and a solid character.

"She's been treated badly her whole life. I can't even imagine all she's endured and survived. By the time I found her, she was almost dead. She'd been abused and had inhaled so much smoke, she was barely hanging onto life. Her recovery has been long and painful, and she still needs some healing time. Mary Ann's constitution is as tough as leather. The Lord only knows how strong she truly is. You need to know she's struggling with being around people and real wary of strange men, especially.

"If I take you to her, you'll have to ease into this idea. Approach her carefully with the notion. You'll need to tread lightly. Take the time to listen to what she has to say."

"Mary Ann, is it?"

"Yes, Mary Ann Barton is her name, and she's young, but you and I both know, in this hard country youth doesn't necessarily factor into what a person is capable of achieving. She's real pretty with long golden-brown hair and big brown, soulful eyes. A man can lose himself in her smile, but she's not used to having many reasons to smile. I don't think I've ever heard her outright laugh. She has scars, both mental and physical scars. She hasn't earned either kind.

"Remarkably, her real, peaceful spirit still shines through when she doesn't feel threatened. If she catches a hint of danger, she shuts down to protect herself. Once you get to know her, the damage isn't too noticeable. Despite all she's suffered, her disposition is like a soft rain. Some people are just sweet, you know, and she's one of those rare people.

"Anyway, I'd seen her around here and there off an' on. She stayed mostly in the shadows of dusk as I made my rounds. I'd only catch glimpses of her. She stayed hidden in the dark, never causing a problem. No one complained, so I just left her to her own business.

"I had no idea how hard things were for her. I'll never forgive myself for not seeing it. It's my job to care about the people in my town, all the people. Mary's had to stay alive on her own ingenuity, being a scavenger, and earning a few pennies doing chores after hours at the schoolhouse. She barely had a grip.

"Now, it makes sense why she was always digging around the trash piles, through other people's discarded things. If she could use it, she took what others no longer wanted. It's likely a few of the kinder women left worn clothes out and a little extra food for her to find if they had it to spare. They tried to help her out of pity. It couldn't have been enough though.

"Where her ma came from is an unanswered question. She died long before I came here. Her pa, BB Barton, has a seedy reputation of drinking, gambling, carousing in the street, stealing, and passing out on walkways in front of businesses. You name it, and he's guilty. Every small town has at least one derelict walking around irritating citizens. The poor feelings for him bled off forming his daughter's reputation by association. The whole town's been wishing they'd both disappear for a long time. The community is happy he's gone now, but mad he didn't take his kin with him.

"This has taught me a hard lesson, Grey, one I'll never forget. I dismissed her as a no-account because of her pa. A town marshal can't be too busy or prejudiced to check on someone. I'm regretful I never made the effort to seek her out and ask the right questions. I sure wish I had."

"How old is she, JD?"

"I'd guess she's seventeen or close. It's hard to tell really. I'll tell you one thing; she's got a sharp head on her shoulders and has educated herself. There will never be anything good for her or the baby here in Spur They need to get away."

Grey soaked up every detail of what JD said. He liked the way her name, Mary Ann, sounded on his tongue. He liked learning she had a sweet temperament.

"Mary Ann, Mary..." He tried the name out several times to familiarize himself with it. He'd not been aware he'd spoken her name out loud until JD broke into his thoughts.

"Yes, Grey, Mary Ann," smiled the marshal.

"I figured she'd be young the way Doc talked about her. It doesn't matter a fig as long as she'll marry me and give my daughter the chance she deserves. Beth was my senior, and I never thought much about our difference in age. It was of no consequence."

Clearing his throat, JD continued. "Like I was saying, this pa of hers is as worthless as a three-legged mule on plowing day. He'll do anything for a coin even if it's illegal. Maybe especially, if it's illegal. I've had to pick him up numerous times for various reasons. He's passed out drunk and hit his head more times than I can count. I pick him up and throw him in jail until he sobers up. At least that's been the pattern until he up and vanished.

"I'd give a month's wages to run across the sorry bastard now. I'd beat him until he talked. I want to know who and where those outlaws are. I've got some choice things to say to BB and questions needin' answers. I'd enjoy beatin' the livin' shit out of him for what he's done to Mary Ann. Maybe he's dead. It's possible the outlaws killed him, but I haven't found a body to prove it.

"He owns a rundown place with a small parcel of land outside of town. There's a house there, more like a shack. Nobody knows how he came to own it, but the bank says he does. It's curious he hasn't sold out for the cash. He ekes out a little spending money from odd jobs and gambling. It's rumored there's a widow woman in another county he works for sometimes. I can't imagine what kind of lady would allow him to hang around her place.

"I can't find any leads on where this nameless woman lives. He disappears for a week or more at a time but never been gone this long before. He's kept quiet about where he goes even when he's drunk as a skunk. I'm wondering if there's more to this affiliation than just being a handyman, illegal activity, maybe."

"What about the card game?" Grey asked. "Doc mentioned something about a bet. What have you found out?"

"I was off with you chasing down those rustlers when the game took place right here in the Side Saddle Saloon. If we hadn't been out looking for them, I might have intervened. When I made it into town with Mary Ann, the very evening of the day you and I parted going our separate ways, there was a lot of buzz about the poker game until I started asking questions. Then the gossipers clammed up and were hesitant to answer my inquiries.

"The doctor in Spur first mentioned the strange story circulating on the street about BB's daughter, three rough men, and a poker game the night I brought her to his office. He hadn't thought much about it until he recognized Mary Ann as BB Barton's girl and put two and two together.

"I forgot about how tired and dirty I was and took to the streets without delay asking questions. Saloons seemed like the most likely place to start the investigation. Bits and pieces of information started coming right away. Some counts were obviously made-up exaggerations. Others were hearsay, but sometimes even those can be helpful to piece a story together. Then there were the actual bits of truth from actual witnesses. Everything started coming together once I made it to the Side Saddle.

"Every recollection pointed to a card game being the crux

of the story. A credible timeline of events formed according to similar, repeated information. I was able to make a list of people to question further at the jailhouse behind a closed door. I only got sketchy descriptions of the suspects because nobody wanted to get involved in case they came back.

"Most of the witnesses were unfortunately three sheets to the wind that night. I took some of what they said with a grain of salt. Business was noisy and hectic during the evening the game took place. The saloon was packed, tables full, and people coming and going from one saloon to another up and down the street. I don't doubt the bartender and working girls are too calloused to see faces anymore, but I don't buy they didn't catch some of what was taking place. More likely, they just aren't forthcoming. They're afraid of being held accountable for not stopping what was happening."

Grey leaned forward in his chair with his elbows supported on his knees and his chin propped up by his fisted hands. "So, what do you think actually happened?"

"There were three men. One stranger was a big, gangly man with large, clumsy hands. He kept dropping his cards on the table and floor like he was nervous. He had one eye covered with a dirty, faded, red bandana wrapped around his head and tied. The cloth was pulled down low covering most of one side above his cheek. His uncovered eye was more centered and a little higher than is normal. Several said it was placed nearly above his nose. He must be a queer-looking man, grotesque even. He shouldn't be hard to identify.

"When Mary Ann was out of her head, she ranted bits and pieces of things about pain, angels, a giant cyclops, somethin' about Polyphemus. The name didn't mean anything to me, but the doctor's wife said it was a reference to Greek Mythology. Her guess was she was referring to a giant with one eye, a cyclops. It matches the description from the saloon.

"She called out for her pa crying and begging him not to

leave her. The distress in her voice nearly broke my heart. It was quite a few days before rest came easier. Doctor kept giving her something to make her sleep. She was out of it for days. When she woke, her memory about what happened was vague, confused and still is. I can't get much useful information from her even now.

"Witnesses said BB played poker most of the evening in a dark corner of the room with three strangers nobody knew. They assumed they were just passing through town. He won a few hands, enough to get him excited and bragging, Then, his luck turned, and he ran out of money.

"The strangers kept pouring free whiskey and urging him to stay in the game anyway. They said he didn't need money if he had somethin' worth puttin' up. Here's where it gets vague. Only a couple of people will admit to thinking BB threw his daughter's name in the pot. The men at the table kept it on the downlow.

"BB was deep in his cups by then and close to passing out. No chance in hell he could win the hand. Little Mary became the property of outlaws. They cleared the table quickly and left with one on each side of Barton, holding him up."

"Are there details about the other two, anything?"

"The name, James, was repeated. Another stood out in the singular way he was dressed all in black with a black silk 'kerchief around his neck. His hat band was silver with small turquoise stones. He may have been a breed, but the lighting was poor.

"Mary Ann thinks there were three or four men and is terrified of the Cyclops she remembers.

"Don't have anythin' else to tell you Grey. I've sent word out on the wire to be on the lookout for them and Barton. I'm hoping a lead will surface."

Grey stored it all in the back of his mind to think about later. Right now, Sari, was the first and foremost.

"Time's not on my side, JD. Doesn't sound like a bad idea

to get Mary away from here. I will convince her to go with me."

CHAPTER 6

G rey caught a couple of hours of sleep before JD's deputy brought breakfast over from the diner just before sunrise. After eating, the two men set out together to see Mary Ann. JD was invested in this girl's welfare. Grey would have better luck talking to Mary with him along.

"Mary Ann is hesitant around strange men and spooks easily. She trusts me and will be right leery of you at first. I don't want her to be frightened."

Adrenaline was pumping through Grey's veins keeping him alert. He had to present himself well and was feeling the pressure building. He and JD rode along in silence for a while.

Then, the marshal finally spoke, "You and I both know Mary really has no choice but to agree to go with you. The decision she makes will rest better with me if she feels like there is a decision to make one way or the other. Don't take her pride too lightly. She's smart too, so be precise in what you say and careful how you handle your words. She'll listen if you're gentle and kind. She'll come around on her own to seeing she has no other choice except to trust you.

"You'll take to her right off, Grey. She's beautiful, brave, and always trying to be independent. Never once have I heard her complain. Her acceptance of the situation she's in has been far beyond my understanding. I envy you, really. Mary Ann is an admirable woman, a rare pearl in this world. Any man would be fortunate to marry her.

"The bottom line working in your favor is the baby she's carrying. If she honestly believes you'll take care of them both it'll tip the scale in your favor. Winter's almost here. Soon she won't be able to take care of herself anymore, and she could use your support. Mary will recognize a better arrangement won't be coming her way."

Grey was becoming very aware of the genuine fondness his friend had for Mary Ann. He could hear it every time he'd spoken of her. JD had a special interest in Mary, but was he sweet on her? His good friend having special feelings for her could make this complicated. He decided to bring it out in the open.

"Friend, do you have feelings for this girl? Come right out and say it if you do."

"Not feelings like you're thinking. No, it's more the guilt for not protecting her before she got hurt. I respect her courage and just really like the person she is. I let Mary down, and I'll never forgive myself. The truth is, I'd like nothing more than someone as decent as you, Grey, to love her. She deserves you for my mistake. She needs to be at Byrd Ranch, have a genuine family, and a secure place to live.

"Grey, to tell the truth, I wouldn't be opposed to marrying her myself, but I can't. The fact is my aunt is sending a bride to me. I've already given my word, and we've already married by proxy. Promises have been made and binding paperwork is signed. She'll be here in the spring. Everything is already in the works, and I've started building a house for us.

"Congratulations, JD, I had no idea. I can't wait to meet your bride." Grey said.

"Thanks, and I'll do anything I can to encourage Mary Ann to marry you. I know for certain you'd take really good care of her and the baby. I'd be happy for them to have a fine home with you and yours. What more could I ever hope for Mary?"

"I'm relieved, because I wouldn't like it a bit to be stepping on your affections, JD. You've eased my mind considerably. If she'll agree to my proposal, be ready to marry us before we head out. You know I'm planning on it happening. I just can't accept no for an answer from her. There's way too much at stake."

Ranger Grey Byrd hadn't supposed he'd be this nervous. The closer he got to meeting her, the more he began to sweat. This took him totally by surprise considering he was usually calm in the face of danger. He'd been in showdowns, tracked outlaws, and stopped robberies but always kept his cool. Not knowing for sure Mary Ann would agree to help him was worrisome. He was about to ask this young woman to marry a stranger and then ride home alone with him.

The confident and compelling words he'd planned to use when pleading his case had dissipated like a vapor in the wind. He couldn't remember any of the logical arguments of persuasion which had come to him so easily during last night's ride. In the dim, sleepy light of dawn, his reservoir was suddenly dried up. His usual confidence was replaced by trepidation and doubt. His mouth was dry, and his tongue felt too big. Praying and giving it over to God was his only hope. God had gotten Sari and him this far, and now he leaned on faith. God is good.

Grey planned to approach Mary Ann Barton humbly and

treat her with honor. He knew he was rushing the girl. It was important she see and hear his sincerity from the very beginning. He would rely on God to open her heart towards him. He prayed she could understand the urgency of Sari's plight and have compassion for his little baby girl. Grey promised himself she'd never regret helping Sari or taking him as a husband.

Mary Ann Barton ◆

Mary Ann began stirring on the hard pallet when pounding commenced at the door. JD's safe and familiar voice swirled around mixing with the fog of her dreams. His knocking was insistent and made quite a racket. He called out to her by name. She, for certain, recognized JD's familiar voice now. Not completely awake, she wondered how long she'd been sleeping. Trying to smooth her mussed hair, she knew her appearance must look a complete mess. It was a silly thought considering the marshal had already seen her at her worst many times. The light in the window was from the sun just coming up. She must have slept from yesterday noon all the way through to this morning. Yet, her body felt lethargic with fatigue and begged for more rest. It took a minute to get her wits gathered and to pull her aching body into a sitting position.

"Mary Ann, Mary Ann, I know you're in there. It's JD, and I brought a friend with me for you to meet. You must talk to him. Open the door for us, Mary Ann."

The knocking became louder and faster.

He brought someone.

She wanted to at least wash her face and comb her hair, but there was no time. She had to open the door and not keep JD and his friend waiting any longer. He'd probably come to remind her about vacating the property. Remembering this sobering thought brought the sad seriousness of her dilemma back to mind. She remembered the dire need to get away. It stoked the fear she had smoldering back to life.

The familiar sense of despair became overwhelming. Worry came rushing back to weigh on her shoulders. An involuntary moan escaped her lips voicing dismay. The problem with sleep is it only brings contentment for the briefest of time. The false peace it offers is most often fleeting. It does nothing to solve real problems.

Her stomach clinched with a dread of the future. The tiny person living within her womb responded in slight movement. Instinctively, she placed a comforting hand on the small mound of her belly. Rising stiffly from the floor with some difficulty, she came up standing as tall as possible. With head held high and shoulders drawn back, she made quick steps to the door. The effort to appear cheery and positive was hard won, but she didn't intend to garner anyone's pity. Yes, she was in a bind, but she'd get it sorted like she did everything else thrown at her.

She was glad JD was here regardless of why he'd come, and even though it was so early. Possibly, he'd found a place for her to go. He'd shown more concern and kindness to Mary Ann these past four months than she'd ever had from anyone else in her life. Because of his friendship, she'd not been totally alone anymore.

Patting her hair down one more time and rubbing as best she could at the crusty sleep in the corners of her eyes, she tried to put a pleasant look on her face. While smoothing the rumpled dress with one hand, she used the other to fumble with the tricky latch. As it released with a metallic clicking and jangling, she pulled on the door. It scraped open to JD's encouraging, warm greeting. Without thinking, she lovingly cradled her stomach. The tall man towering over JD a short distance behind him gave her pause.

She wiped a cheek with her fingertips stalling for time. Strangers were more worrisome since the attack. JD would not allow harm to come to her by bringing a threat to the door. Though curious, she managed not to scrutinize the nameless cowboy. She had concerns as to why he was here but kept them to herself for now.

The new light of day behind the men was partially obstructed by the stranger's imposing size. His height and bulk blocked it from reaching beyond the doorway. It made both men appear as darkened silhouettes. Mary Ann angled her head back farther trying to get a better view of the stranger's face. Her curious gaze traveled downward but got no farther than the badge he was wearing.

Her voice faltered as she addressed JD. "Uh, Marshal, what brings you here this morning? If it's about me leaving, I promise you, I'll be gone by this afternoon. I'm guessing you came to remind me of the deadline for clearing out. I already assured the banker I'd go without a fuss."

"Where're you planning to go, Mary?"

"I'm still deciding and haven't made up my mind yet."

JD was a good-looking man, but his companion was taller and strikingly handsome. She wanted to get a better look at his face but couldn't be caught staring. His hands were fidgeting with the hat he held just below his belted waist. He was slowly twirling it, and the constant motion drew her attention. His clothing was dusty, but not grimy, and he hadn't shaved lately. The short hairs made an intriguing shadow on his face.

His eyes were entirely focused on her face. She felt self-conscious and lacking under his appraisal. Now, he was specifically working the hat brim rolling it between his fingers. For some reason she remembered her own disheveled state and began fidgeting also. She pushed and tucked stray strands of hair away from her face. She couldn't fathom why she cared what this man thought of her. She didn't need or desire his approval.

The answer she'd given JD's question had been spoken with more certainty than she felt. It wasn't a lie, really, but it was skirting around the truth. She had nowhere to go unless she gave in and returned to Pa's house. She was still trying to think of another alternative. She doubted the feigned good spirits of her words reached her eyes. It wouldn't fool JD. There was no way he hadn't seen through her play acting but was too polite to call her bluff in front of the stranger.

Greyson Byrd ✦

The run-down homestead was depressing and silent. It looked deserted as Grey followed JD's horse into the sparse yard. Leaving the horses ground tied, the two men mounted the loose porch boards. He hung back letting JD take the lead while he observed. JD knocked several times while rattling the door, and he called out the girl's name. He identified them so she wouldn't be startled when she saw he'd brought someone she didn't know to the doorstep.

JD hadn't exaggerated one iota when he'd said she was pretty. It was an understatement. Even in her drowsy and rumpled state, Mary Ann Barton was a looker with long, thick, golden-brown hair falling well past her shoulders and framing her face. She was so gaunt her slenderness alarmed Grey. Where there should have been soft curves on a woman, the lack of weight exposed the sharp angles of her frame. None-the-less, she was appealing, but it was concerning to see her pale, waxy skin with not a hint of rose in her cheeks.

He saw something else too. Mary Ann Barton's eyes were rimmed with unshed tears when JD asked her where she'd decided to go. He knew from all JD had shared, this young lady had no one or anywhere to go for shelter. His heart strings were tugged by the multitude of needs and worries she was facing. The urge to reach out and offer his support then and there was strong. The desire to protect this small woman was overpowering.

The jolt of awareness initially hitting him when she opened the door had caught him completely off guard. He'd been bombarded by so many unfamiliar feelings in the past three days he couldn't trust his own mind, already knowing her story had filled him with empathy. He thought he knew just what to expect, but he'd not been prepared for Mary Ann Barton. This brave girl was more than just a means to an end. She really did need him, Sari, and a home of her own. She didn't know yet, but he was determined to give her all of it.

Miss Barton's malnourished body needed food and rest. Her translucent skin was in sharp contrast to the darkened slivers of half-moons lying under her eyes. He couldn't wait to feed her all she could eat and tuck her into a soft bed. He'd never been hungry a day in his life, and it made him sad to think hunger was all she'd ever known. The thought of her and her baby starving tore him apart inside.

JD was right when he warned him not to bruise her fierce pride. She was a warrior standing straight and tall in the throes of adversity. When Mary Ann's eyes locked with his challenging stare, he immediately found great admiration for her. The way her hands, lovingly cradled her belly spoke of the fine mother she already was and would be.

The desire to rescue her made his chest tighten with resolve. He had to convince her to let him do so. He would readily take responsibility for her and the baby. He was surprised to feel so much compassion for this woman when they hadn't even exchanged words. She was the one who belonged with Sari and him.

God, please let her agree to leave with me.

CHAPTER 7

―――――◆◈◆―――――

Greyson Byrd ◆

"**M**ary Ann, this is a good friend of mine, Ranger Grey Byrd. He owns a big spread around Cap Rock."

Hearing JD speak his name put a stop to Grey's woolgathering. He was being called front and center to the stage. This was his chance to state his case.

"He's come a long way just to see you, Mary. This isn't official business. It's more of a social call of a personal nature. I think you should listen carefully to what he has to say and think about what he's suggesting carefully. He has something to offer very much worth considering. His words will be truthful. His words are always spoken in truth. You can trust him, I promise. I wouldn't have brought him here otherwise."

They entered the sparse cabin when she stepped back and invited them in. Grey stood nervously, with hat in hands, until she motioned for them all three to take a seat at the small table.

"Miss Barton, Ma'am, I'm a rancher like JD said. I'm also

a Texas Ranger right now, but I don't plan on being one for much longer. Today, I'm coming to you as simply a man with a wagon load of responsibilities and very little time. I'm going to ask for your help to smooth out the challenges I'm facing. In return, I'm going to explain how I can be of help to you with the things you're needing. I'll lay it all out, so please, bear with me. We both are walled in by unfortunate happenings."

Mary Ann's curiosity was piqued, and the man had her attention. She waited patiently for him to get started.

"I rode all night from Garza County to be here this mornin' to meet with you. I need to start back within the hour if possible. I have heard of your misfortunes and your present circumstances. JD told me you are a fine woman caught up in some troubles like I am. Due to time restrictions, I'm forced to be more direct and blunter than I'd normally be. I'll try not to be too indelicate, but please forgive me if I overstep."

She glanced at JD for reassurance.

The marshal nodded his head before he spoke. "His spread is a big, beautiful place. I've been there, Mary Ann, many times. Grey's kin are the nicest people you'd ever want to meet. He's already told me what he's going to ask. I agreed to introduce the two of you. I think he has some good ideas and solutions to benefit both of you. Grey coming here is a fine thing, actually."

She looked to Grey again and bobbed her chin for him to continue.

"I'll get right down to the meat of it, then. My wife died in childbirth three days ago." He looked away for a moment regrouping his thoughts before continuing. "Our baby girl lived, but she's not doing well. She's going to die soon if I can't get what she needs."

Mary's sweet face frowned before she said to him, "I'm sorry to hear of your wife, Mr. Byrd. You must be hurting. I can't imagine such heavy sorrow."

The gentle sound of her voice touched him. Her thoughtful words, considering the mess she was trying to dig through, humbled Grey. The way she was giving him a moment of privacy by studying the wood grain of the table and tracing it with a fingernail showed kindness, in his mind.

"This crisis I'm experiencing concerns my baby girl, Sari, Sari Elizabeth. Miss Barton, the milk, every kind we've tried to give her, has been rejected. She can't keep any of it down. Cow's milk won't suit, so I borrowed a milk goat, and she can't keep its milk down either. Doc says she's got to have a mother's milk and, of course, as soon as possible.

"There's no wet nurse to be had or not one who can help anyway. Your name was suggested to me yesterday afternoon, and I came to find you right away. If you'll help Sari eat, I'll help you with everything you need in return. We can fight each other's battles together, as a team.

"I know about your present condition. Our two lives have been shattered by events beyond our control. We're both struggling alone to put the broken pieces back together. Neither of us can be successful without the other's help. I want to help you as much as I want you to help me.

"I came to ask you to join forces with me. It's a workable solution for both of us and both of our babies. We might as well be broken together and fix whatever's wrong. We each have things to contribute. We'll raise our children on the ranch and do what's best for them. We'll be parents together and make a home where they can grow up safe, happy with a mother and a father."

She lowered her shoulders slightly, putting her elbows on the table and rubbing her temples with her fingertips. "I'm hearing your plans but am confused," Mary Ann sighed. "How can we be of help to each other with these entirely different problems?"

Her face flushed, and she gave a soft, little whimper. Observing her body language and without thinking, Grey reached out touching her arm to console her. He felt her flinch slightly and withdrew his contact. He'd clearly startled her. The soft, sound of distress she'd made had been his undoing. He'd frightened her with his contact.

"There's no need to be afraid of me, Miss Barton. I want only to help both of us get back on our feet. A heinous crime put you where you are now, and an unfortunate loss has put me here with you today. Don't feel shame for yourself or pity for me. We neither had the power to stop what happened to us. I've had experiences with innocent victims of evil men, and I've observed it's always the ones who accept help who survive disasters best. We owe it to our children to reach out to each other.

"Harsh winter weather is ahead. Don't try to face it by yourself without me. You must have a roof over your head, food to eat, a warm fire, and good people around you. Allow me to give you a home, a family, security, everything, and anything. I'm offering you immediate answers to your problems. My protection is yours for the taking.

"You and your infant must get away from here today. You must leave Spur behind. I understand how people in small towns think. They can be cruel. Without a husband you'll both be shunned and mistreated. You and your child can't stay here. Think of your sweet baby. Your child will be ostracized if you don't leave. Go with me.

"I promise you, Miss Barton, I'll see the men who hurt you held accountable for what they've done. I'll bring them to justice before I turn in my badge, I swear. I'll dog their trails until they're all found. They will pay for hurting you! They'll know you are mine."

After Grey finished pouring his heart out, Mary Ann sat still as a stone for a long moment. Her face was without expression. Her eyes looked off into the distance. He had no way of reading her thoughts. He could only wait with no idea what she was going to say next. Tension grew thick in the little house and hung like a cloud over the table.

Finally, she spoke. "JD says you're a good person, Mr.

Byrd. I've learned to trust his judgement. I know he wants what's best for me. He vouches for your good, dependable, and honest character. I would be lying if I said I don't need your help. I believe you are a good man. You deserve for Sari to live, and I want to help her, but I don't understand how all of this can work."

She searched JD's face. The marshal gave Mary an encouraging smile and another nod. She knew JD would not lead her into trouble. There might be hope harmony was within her reach.

"What exactly do you want of me? What are you suggesting I do, Mr. Byrd?"

Her question gave him confidence. He felt he could take a deep breath for the first time in three days. He gave her a smile and a thoughtful look. Grey measured his response carefully.

"We each have babies who need both parents. My baby lies dying of hunger as we speak. She needs a mother to feed her, love her, take care of her, and raise her. She needs you to be her mother. You need a good man to claim you and your newborn. You need a husband to give you both his name and provide for you. You both need family, love, and protection. It would be an honor to be the man who takes care of you. Let's agree on an arrangement, a bargain of sorts.

"Let's settle things between us. I apologize for not having time for us to get acquainted properly, but we need to get married today and then leave for the ranch. Doc says pregnancy will allow you to produce milk. You'll be able to nurse Sari."

"Mr. Byrd, I've been praying night and day for a way to provide for my baby and trade my miseries for a better life. I yearn for a safe, warm shelter to winter, a bed to rest in, plenty of food, and a brighter future. Yes, I need a husband and a home. I want a home. I am open to the agreement you're proposing. I knew God would provide, but you are a surprise, Mr. Byrd."

Grey smiled and agreed. "It's a fine thing we're doing, Mary Ann. You won't be sorry, I promise. I regret rushing you around, but we must get started for home as soon as possible. My sister-in-law, Belle, is tending Sari now with a special broth concoction Doc suggested. She told me when I left yesterday not to come back without you. She'll be expecting us and have a room all ready for you.

"The ranch is about twenty-five miles west of here if we travel as the crow flies. Cross country is rough traveling, but it cuts off some time, and I have an excellent, sure-footed horse. If we leave soon, we can make it back before dusk.

"JD can legally marry us before we head out, Mary Ann Barton. It'll give you security in my promises, and things will be proper between us.

"I'll only expect you to take care of Sari and yourself under my, our, roof for the time being. We'll get to know each other and after the baby is born, we can work on having a real marriage. We'll figure things out together as we go along.

"How old are you, Mary Ann?"

"I'm sixteen but will be seventeen soon. How about you?"

"Twenty-seven and the age difference will work," Grey assured her.

"I'm not a poor man, Mary. My ranch does well. You'll have plenty to eat and whatever else you need or want. I'll never let anyone disrespect or hurt you or your baby. I swear to it.

"One thing though you should remember, I loved my wife. I am sorely grieving her passing. It will take me a while to come to terms with it, but I will make room in my heart for you. I feel Beth looking down from heaven and giving us her blessing."

"As soon as Marshal JD marries us, you can gather your things and we'll head out. We're both doing the right thing for each other."

CHAPTER 8

---◆-❖-◆---

James, Frank, and Arliss ◆

T he three outlaws, James, Frank, and Arliss rode in a line headed straight for the rugged canyons of Palo Duro. It had been a mistake to lust after BB Barton's girl and cheat him. It was only by chance she escaped the fire Arliss had set and lived to talk about what happened. It was worse luck her marshal friend took up her cause and was relentless in tracking them down. He had every lawman in Texas looking for them. Interest in their hides had risen to sizeable dollar amounts. Every unsolved murder and crime in the territory had suddenly been put on their heads. All it took to claim the rewards was their bloody heads in gunny sacks. Wanted posters were nailed on every post and tree overnight. They were wanted Dead or Alive.

The sharp ridges, ravines, gullies, and deep gorges would be the safest place to lie low until things cooled off. With any luck the law and bounty hunters would give up and move on, but the Texas Rangers wouldn't let go so easily. Once the rangers caught an outlaw's scent, they wouldn't let go. The men's horses were packed with provisions enough to last for quite a while. Keeping out of sight was the only hope at staying alive. It was safer than running out in the open.

They rode in silence until Arliss started his irritating whining. The other two groaned at losing the peace and quiet. Common sense, logic, and backbone were non-existent with him. He'd have to go sooner or later, but for right now he made a damn good slave. He could be tricked and bullied into doing anything. As a bonus, the idiot was a first-rate arsonist. Arliss loved to set fires.

"James, James, what about them papers on our heads? Wha'd the words say again? Ya' know I can't read."

"The writing, Arliss? The words say you'll be hunted down like a cur dog and hung by your neck until your boots fall off, your feet quit shakin,' an' yer plum' dead. This is what will happen only if you're taken alive. You might just be killed, have your head cut off on the spot, an' it'll end up being delivered to the nearest sheriff's office for the reward. If you don't shut up about it, I'll turn yer head in myself."

Arliss may have been simple-minded and of little use except for three skills. He was downright creative when it came to administering torture, causing pain, and he was enthralled by flames. Though his simple mentality grated on the nerves of James and Frank, his twisted and bizarre appetites were helpful now and then. Setting a good fire delighted the man. He was a firebug and excelled in his skill. In fact, he was a genius at burning things up. He had gotten them away from several towns unnoticed with fires. Nothing occupies the attention of townsfolk like burning houses, barns, and businesses. How he did get off on hot, crackling flames and screaming!

"Awwwww! I don't wanna lose my head or get strung up neither. It's good we're leavin', ain't it? Ain't it? We'll make it won't we? We just get caught up in the excitement sometimes. We's just havin' a little fun. Don't mean nothin' purs-nal by it.

"Oh, Lord, have mercy! Lord, please have mercy on us!

He sounded like he might start crying. He'd done it before. Without looking back at the pathetic man, James barked, "You're peculiar as shit. Don't go getting religion on me, Arliss. It's way late for God to help ya'! Ya' can't sniffle' your way out a' anythin'!

"Ya' best realize, if'n there's a God, He won't cut the likes of ya' any last-minute deals. Yer done too late fer savin.' Ya' best be 'memberin' how yer eye got popped out of its socket. You could still be hung for it an' plenty a' other things too. The best ya can do now is shut up and ride hard. Put miles between ya an' the men comin' up from behind. Once we reach the canyons, nobody'll find us."

Not satisfied, Arliss called ahead to the stone-sullen man in black sitting up straight and regal on his horse. "Frank, what say ya'll? What do ya' think on hangin'?"

I swear I'll slit the bastard's throat from ear to ear the first chance I get.

Frank growled, "Shut up ya' pervert. Shut your damn mouth. Shut it! I'm warning you! I'll cut a grin right below your chin to match the hole in your head."

That was the most consecutive words the surly man, who kept to himself, had spoken in a month of Sundays. Anytime he bothered to speak it was a noteworthy occasion. Frank spit on the ground sealing his promise of violence he'd just made against Arliss.

BB Barton ✦

BB Barton wasted no time in getting his cowardly hide out of Spur. The very night he betrayed Mary Ann was the night he left. The marshal was due back in town any day now, and he didn't plan on being around to answer his questions. BB had a bad feeling about how all this was going to turn out for him. He didn't specifically know what the three men had planned to do to Mary, but he did know they were very vile men. He'd be blamed for any harm coming to her.

As soon as he dropped the girl off, he knew the shit had piled up deeper than he could wade through. They'd roughed him up good the night before motivating the turncoat to meet their demands. He genuinely believed they'd kill him if he didn't do exactly as he was told. To save his own skin, he had no other choice but to do exactly as he was instructed. Once he'd delivered the girl, he'd wiped his hands with relief and got away fast. He didn't even know who the men were exactly but was sure she would have been better off dropped into a den of rattlesnakes.

How'd I get myself into another fine mess?

The only safe place to go was back to Cap Rock and hold up in the crazy-mean lady's barn. He'd lie low for as long as it took for the heat to cool. Spinster Winters wouldn't be happy to see him show up unannounced, but he'd hold black mail over her head. She'd come around to his way of thinking and be submissive. He knew too much about the murders she'd committed because he'd helped her conceal them. The old bitty had a hunger for poisoning people. With what he knew about her herb business, he had enough details to nail her murdering grits to the wall.

She was a cold-blooded killer, and she paid him well to do her clean-up work. There'd been times she'd coerced him into doing things making his skin crawl, but the pay was too considerable to pass up. If a job was especially messy, there was always a hefty bonus attached. She'd hide, feed him, and do whatever else he wanted to keep him quiet. He was sure of it.

The cheeky female was a smug one, but she couldn't risk him going to the law with details of the secret garden, her private laboratory, or the location of victims' bodies. He could show them the buried corpses and the ones dumped in the well. She'd be ruined if he told what had happened to a single vanishing drunk, vagrant, or missing drummer over the years. She'd let him hide in the barn all right, and he'd only come out after dark so nobody would see him. No one had ever seen him on her property before and wouldn't suspect he was there this time either. BB would stay hidden to keep the nosey marshal in Spur from finding him.

He'd go back home to Mary Ann once things were forgotten. He didn't care about the girl in the least. She'd always been a yoke around his neck. She was of no worth to him except for the monetary value of the house and the land deed being in her name. She didn't know, and it was in his best interest not to tell her. The deed had been sealed by her real father before she was born. The high and mighty businessman from long ago wanted nothing to do with his bastard child.

It couldn't be opened until she requested it to be unsealed. The yearly taxes were kept paid anonymously, and nobody ever showed up in person to pay them. If Mary Ann knew the power, she held over him, he'd lose the house and land in a heartbeat. Resentment of her control made beating Mary Ann feel so much better. He loved hearing her beg him to stop as she cried. Her mother had made the same racket when he'd finally beaten her to death.

Damn her ma for causing all the trouble he'd suffered! The whore had screwed with the wrong man. When he got her pregnant, she, the baby, and the homestead had been dropped into BB's lap as a packaged deal. At the time, it seemed to be tied together by a silky ribbon and was too much to be refused. He signed an agreement to take the woman and infant as his own. He kept his mouth shut in trade for a cash settlement and a roof over his head. Her ma knew the truth of it and threatened to tell Mary as soon as she got older. He'd blown out her candle before she had the chance.

Mary Ann had to stay alive. There was a stipulation in the deed reverting everything back to the original benefactor if she died. He'd been stuck with her, and she was a rotting, stinking carcass around his neck.

BB had been trying to recollect how the men had tricked

him into giving up the girl, but his mind had been cloudy with whiskey. He couldn't quite grasp all of what transpired. He'd just been paid on the day before by the Winters woman. He knew the money would have been burning a hole in his pocket. In the afternoon he would have been three sheets to the wind because he could afford a bottle. He didn't remember any of this, but his routine on payday was always the same. He'd sit against the wall in a dark alley slugging the liquid down and dozing off until the saloons got noisy.

There was a card game, but there was always a card game. The memory of this one seemed hazier than usual. Cowhands and transient drifters were typically crowded into the dark saloons, spirits high, and the tunes of tinny pianos spilling out the doors. He remembered the noises being louder than they should have been. He could almost feel how hard his heart thumped against the wall of his chest. He remembered a fierce headache. The men at the table got to laughing pushing him to consume more and more drinks. He thought they were just being friendly. The roar of the crowd pulsed painfully in his head matching the pounding of his heart.

The rip-roaring chaos confused him. Everyone looked like they were leaning to one side. The drinks were strong. How he'd ended up in a dark alley with his head in the dirt, he never knew. He could still smell the pee-soaked earth and feel the rhythm in his head.

He couldn't forget getting hit in the face, punched in the gut, and puking on his boots. The sharp pains had cleared his head somewhat which was unfortunate because there was so much pain. He tried to get away, but the effort was useless. A man said they'd seen his pretty little daughter and wanted her. BB had to bring her to them, or he'd regret it. The man had BB repeat his instructions over and over. He was to take her to the house south of town the next afternoon and make sure he wasn't followed. He had to leave as soon as he got her there. They'd kill him if he didn't do it just like he was told.

He had believed they would.

CHAPTER 9

Mary Ann Barton Byrd ✦

G rey and Mary Ann married quietly with no fanfare. When JD came to the part about a kiss, Grey put a light touch of his lips to her forehead. Considering the spirit of their contract, it was a proper gesture. He apologized to his bride for not having a ring. She hadn't expected there would be one, so she hadn't given it a thought. She was thankful enough to be spared certain hardships. She'd gotten up this morning under the gloom of desperation. Only a short time later, she was entertaining a feeling of hope. So, once again it was proven true, nothing is impossible for God.

Grey and JD talked outside while she gathered her few belongings. The meager possessions fit easily into a flour sack knotted at the top. She had a faded bonnet the old lady had left behind, and she tied it under her chin. Head held down submissively, she shut the door to her past. She was choosing to place her trust in the handsome ranger and his great, white stallion.

Grey caught her chin up between his thumb and index

finger lifting her head until they were eye-to-eye. She was feeling shy of this stranger who was her husband, but he was unaccepting of her sudden shyness. It was a fact she had no example of what being married entailed. His gesture presented a bridge allowing her to cross the myriad of emotions threatening to hold her back.

"Mary Ann, you weren't gone but a minute. Are you sure you didn't leave something behind? We can afford you a few more minutes to go back inside and check."

In answer, she simply held up the flour sack for him to take from her. It held the only earthly belongings she had. The Bible and a locket, both left by a mother she hardly remembered, were the most important things. The delicate gold locket held a tiny image of the woman she called Mama framed in one side. On the other, was a man who'd never had a name. His identity had always been a mystery.

There was also a Greek Mythology tome from the teacher at the school, her slingshot, a comb with missing teeth, a chunk of stale bread, and a rubbery, sprouting sweet potato. This was the sum of what she owned. Meager as the contents of the bag were, the items told a story to anyone who cared to examine them.

She understood the difference between the two books. She'd read the Bible and studied it from cover to cover. The Greek stories were entertaining and spurred her imagination, but stories in the Bible were real and full of truths. The myths were just made-up tales about the sky, flying horses, heroes, villains and how everything under the sun came to be. There was no truth in this book, but there were insights to ponder. The ranger tied the sack onto the back of the great white horse, no further mention was made of her belongings.

Grey mounted first, reaching down to lift Mary up as JD kindly assisted her up toward her husband's open arms. There she was on top of the Pegasus, the white and mighty mythical steed. The horse made her think of the winged Pegasus in the myths, and in her mind from this day forward, it became the animal's name. Grey settled her in front of him across his lap with her legs dangling to one side. He wrapped his strong arms around her and held the reins in one hand. She felt self-conscious but was anchored and safe in his arms.

Her friend, JD, offered his hand in farewell to her and said, "Mary Ann Byrd, I want all the happiness you've missed out on to be yours now. Look forward and don't be afraid to enjoy life. Grey will take good care of you and your baby, or he'll have to answer to me. Going with him is the right choice. Let him take care of your worries for a change. I'll get over to the ranch soon and check on you."

Mary Ann nodded her head and smiled at her friend. "You've been good to me, Marshal. I thank you kindly. Please tell the doctor and his wife where I've gone and thank them for helping me too."

The men shook hands bidding each other goodbye, and she was carried away to a new home and future on the wings of Pegasus.

The man, Grey Byrd, was real and this was no fairytale written in a book. It was real life as it was happening. The motion of his hand reaching into the front of his shirt captured Mary's attention. He withdrew a small parcel wrapped in cloth and offered it to her.

"I know you haven't eaten today because you were still sleeping when JD knocked on the door. You need food, Mary, and I know you're hungry. Eat. There's always more. Always, you may have more."

She could smell the food, and her mouth watered in anticipation. Under the cloth, she found a buttered biscuit sandwich filled with sweet, cured ham. Her eyes opened wide, and she could hardly contain her excitement. She'd never been given such a fine treat. It smelled like the outside of the cafe in town whenever the door was opened. She looked up, and he was waiting for her to bite into it. He nodded his head encouraging her to enjoy the nourishment.

"Go on and eat. I've got another like it as soon as this one is gone."

Indecision was written on her face. His expression became stern, so she hurried to do his bidding. Putting the biscuit cautiously to her mouth, she sampled it, taking only a small nibble.

"Come on now. You can do better than that for me. Take a decent bite. You need to eat for you and both babies, Mary Ann. I told you there's plenty more where this came from. I will always provide food for you and our family."

After the taste, a strong urge to stuff the whole thing into her mouth at once was almost more than she could put off. She'd been hungry for so long. There had never been enough. She allowed herself to take a genuine bite. Then she indeed had trouble holding back. In her eagerness, the biscuit and meat were gone far too soon. She licked and inspected every finger not allowing a single morsel to go to waste.

He laughed, but not at her. It was good natured sound, a pleased laugh of delight. He handed her a second parcel like the first, and this time he didn't have to coax.

"It brings me pleasure to see you eat, but two sandwiches are enough for now. Your stomach is not used to rich food, but soon it will adjust. Being hungry will become a distant memory. It breaks my heart to think of you struggling so hard to scrape together what I've always taken for granted. You've lived a hard life, but today, it will start getting better. I'm ashamed to have taken so many blessings for granted. My feeling of entitlement stops today too. You've already started making me into a better man."

After the second buttered biscuit with ham, the girl's thin body wilted in fatigue. She hadn't relaxed her body to lean on his yet because it seemed too intimate. Now, she was fighting to keep her eyes open. The second time she jerked to consciousness from the edge of sleep, Grey had enough of the nonsense.

"Rest against me, Mary Ann. Lean back and put your

weight on me." The way he said it booked no argument, but when she did not move in compliance, he continued more emphatically. "You're tired and need rest. Let me be your bed to sleep upon. I won't let you fall. I'll never let you fall. I'll guard you from harm. Trust me in this."

He gently guided her to lie back against his hard chest. She gave into the slight pressure easily because she was so tired. His warmth combined with the satisfied feeling of fullness easily lured her. Soon, she was fast asleep as Pegasus continued to eat up the miles.

CHAPTER 10

Greyson Byrd ✦

W ith the girl asleep, Grey was left with his own thoughts. Naturally, regardless of the reasons, he'd been apprehensive to commit to a speedy marriage immediately following the burial of his wife. Faith and love for his child necessitated this action, but once JD related Mary Ann's history, he began to think of this spot in time differently. Except for Sari's life and death emergency, Mary Ann Barton was stuck in a world more ravaged than his. He'd believed JD's account of how sweet and kind she remained in the center of constant adversity. He'd been most curious to meet such an exceptional person.

He would always love Beth, no doubt about it, but a powerful desire to save not one but two babies had engulfed him. Grey was playing a part in three miracles from God. One in his life, one saving Sari's life, and one changing the lives of Mary Ann and her blameless infant. He, a selfish and self-centered man, was being gifted the rare chance to get things right. This time around he'd focus on being a better husband and a good father. Sari was being given the opportunity to experience life and love against all odds. Mary and her child were being taken from a certain existence of hardships and suffering.

Bearing the weight of this young woman felt natural. Witnessing her finally relaxing made him happy to take her home where she could eat, rest, and quit fretting. Having to fight the world alone was over. No one would harm her again. He'd do his best for his new wife and children.

Grey nudged the horse to pick up the pace. This journey would take a toll on Mary Ann's already weakened body. The ranger instinctively tucked her closer to minimize the effects of the constant jarring. It was fortunate she could sleep, but her muscles would still stiffen and ache from the motion of the ride. Moving around when they stopped for a break would help. The horse needed a chance to graze and drink from the creek.

Later, he pulled him to a stop causing Mary Ann to stir. Dismounting, he helped her down from the horse. Not fully awake yet, he held her upright until her legs could support her.

"I'll water the horse and see to him. You need to walk around while you can. This trip is wearing on you, and we're less than half-way home. Don't wander off too far. I'll go off in the opposite direction to give you privacy."

She nodded but came short of making eye contact. He guessed it was going to take time for her to be comfortable around him. He watched her unsteady steps as she walked away. She took them cautiously at first until she found her legs, and he was satisfied. She headed toward the line of trees and brush he'd suggested.

When she returned from making her ablutions, Grey had taken a big red apple from his saddle bags. He held it out to her. She took it carefully in both hands and examined it from every angle. She rubbed her thumbs over the smooth skin and smelled of it with a slow intake of breath while her eyes were closed. A soft smile curled her lips. He was fascinated by her unabashed pleasure in studying the fruit. When she handed it back to him, Grey didn't know what to think.

"No," he assured her. "This apple is for you, but I can cut it if you like."

"I couldn't. It wouldn't be right to eat this whole apple by myself. I want you to have some of it," she insisted softly.

Grey ran his eyes over the wafer-thin girl before him and pulled his pocketknife out of his pants. Obviously, this fruit was something special, but it was in her nature to share. It amazed him. Expertly, he sliced a thin wedge from the juicy apple. He gently and deliberately brought it to her lips. The succulent, juicy fragment was balanced on the blade and held in place by a calloused thumb. Her soft lips parted and accidently touched his skin as she plucked it from him. He felt like he was feeding a little bird and a barely noticeable flicker of something buzzed through him.

Closing her eyes, she chewed slowly and deliberately making the sliver last. A drop of the juice spilled down her lower lip. A pink tongue darted out catching it. Her movements were the most provocative sights he'd ever seen, and she innocently showed no awareness of what she was doing. Watching her eat was riveting. Grey would remember this later as the exact moment Mary started easing her way into his heart.

She waited patiently for the next bite causing a chuckle to escape Grey, and she smiled making eye contact fleetingly. He repeated cutting slices, one at a time, until he'd handfed her every morsel of the apple, but the core which he let her feed to his horse. He'd been observing her with devoted interest the entire time. She'd been so engrossed in the process of eating she hadn't acknowledged he was staring.

Breaking the spell, Mary Ann whispered, "But, Mr. Byrd, you didn't take any for yourself."

"No, Ma'am, I didn't, and call me Grey," he said. "You need this sustenance way more than I do. Believe me, I enjoyed every bite you took. I'm privileged to have given you all of it. When we get to the ranch, you can have as many apples as you can eat along with other fruits and vegetables of every sort. You can have milk and buttermilk from your own cows to drink every day.

"My, our, sister-in-law, Belle, makes cakes, pies, puddings, and cookies often. She bakes fresh bread every other day. It fills the whole house with a warm aroma. There is butter and jam to put on the warm bread, as much as you like. The ranch produces home-grown beef, chickens, eggs, ham, and lots of other things to eat.

Grey mused what had just transpired between them. They'd had a conversation. It was a first. He took four slices of buttered bread out of his saddlebags. To this he added thick pieces of roast beef and made them each a sandwich. While she ate this, he re-saddled Snow. He mounted, reaching down to pull Mary across his lap again. She was light as a feather. She moaned slightly when her sore bottom met his hard, muscled legs.

He could barely hear the evidence of her discomfort, but he knew she was bruised from sitting and being jostled. There was nothing to do for it because he had to get back to Sari. After eating half of his own sandwich, he feigned disinterest and passed the remaining portion to her. She accepted his offering without arguing this time. When she finished his leftover piece, they swigged cool, fresh creek water from the canteen.

Grey's thoughts were building at the awkward idea of bringing a new wife into Beth's house. It didn't quite set right but knowing Sari would benefit helped a lot. He wasn't ready for his family to suspect he already cared for Mary Ann. He couldn't keep from feeling shame. With it came the recollection of standing at Beth's grave and asking her what to do. Using Doc, she'd led him straight to Mary Ann. It had been an immediate answer solving a serious problem. It was a gift from God. A calming peace washed over him. It was as crystal clear as a warm spring rain. Faith filled him with assurance, and he'd not question the wisdom of this miracle again.

In the distance, the township of Cap Rock came into view. Structures scattered here and there, and other silhouettes popped into view as they rode closer. He could feel tension in Mary's body building as she was seeing the town. Grey pulled the horse to a stop and lifted her chin. He directed her head around slightly, until she could look at him.

"Calm down, Mary. Breathe, you hear me? We won't be stopping in town today. We have about three more miles before we reach the house. Sari needs us at home without delay. You will only see the family tonight. The Lord knows they'll be glad to see you. They've all been worrying about their niece. Don't fret because I'll keep you close to me. Can you try to calm down?

"Use words and let me know you understand. I'll be with you the whole time. Nobody will bother you. I'm going to keep reminding you of how safe you are until you accept it. You're under my protection, and my brothers will back me up if trouble comes."

She nodded and responded with a barely audible yes. Grey accepted her one-word answer as a start.

CHAPTER 11

Belle Byrd ✦

Belle Byrd was reeling from the loss of her only friend in the world. More than a sister-in-law, Beth was like the big sister she'd never had. When Smith first brought her to the ranch, Beth made room under her wing to nurture and teach Belle the rudiments of managing a home and caring for family. Thanks to her patience, Belle mastered the skills of homemaking. In fact, she found she had a knack for it. Beth was one of those extraordinary souls God puts on the earth to encourage others.

The funeral had been a fitting tribute to the woman who was loved by so many in the community. Grey sat serenely throughout the service showing no outward emotion. Struggling with disbelief and shock, he'd not been the confident Grey everyone knew. This tragedy had happened so intensely and too swiftly to fathom. His two younger brothers gave him their support, and Belle stayed by his side. Grey let her know in private Wisteria was not welcomed to sit with the family today. Belle had no qualms in shielding him from the woman's caustic mouth and manners.

By the time the preacher directed the guests into the house for the reception, Belle imagined steam coming out of Wisteria's ears. She'd put on quite the show of playing the role of a broken-hearted cousin all morning. Belle had reasons to suspect she was not the individual she tried to mirror. The benevolent, devoted character she projected was more likely only an illusion. It was very possible she'd had a hand in Beth's death, but Belle didn't have enough proof to accuse her yet.

Today's performance was overdone but flawless as usual, right down to pretending to swoon. Belle observed her picking a position logistically, so Grey was in the right place to step forward and catch her easily. To Wisteria's chagrin, he turned his back to talk with a neighbor just as she was on the way down.

Good for Grey!

One of the ranch hands caught her at the last second just before she smacked into the floor. She made a remarkably quick recovery. She gathered up her things, announcing she was just too distraught to stay longer. Few acknowledged her early departure, and conversations continued uninterrupted.

What a phony!

Beth had been buried no more than an hour, and this wicked woman was already walking around trying to steal the stage from her. Wisteria wanted all to believe she was heartbroken, but Belle didn't buy it. The woman was a fraud, and Belle was determined to tear away her cover. Somehow, she would expose the wickedness she concealed from Beth's family and friends.

Two days prior, Beth had been acutely overcome with a violent intestinal spell. The other episodes she'd experienced prior to this last one had paled in comparison. The stomach pains were unbearable, and her screams raised the hair on the heads of those who heard them. Belle ran to be of help immediately. She was entering the door of the bedroom just as Wisteria was telling Beth unkindly to shut up.

"Shut up, Beth! You'll bring everyone within a mile running. Be still now. Why must you take on so? You've never been anything but a burr under my saddle!"

Belle had backed out of the room before Wisteria was aware of her presence. She returned making more noise this time. Had she known Beth was dying, she would have rattled Wisteria's teeth and gotten the truth out of her.

As destiny insisted, Doc showed up without warning finding Beth in the throes of misery. It was not uncommon for him to make a house call unexpectedly to check on Beth since none of her prior pregnancies had gone well. Strangely, as he came in, Wisteria disappeared. Doc and Belle were busy with Beth, and there was a great deal of commotion. It went unnoticed she'd fled the ranch entirely until later.

It was only by chance Grey had ridden in shortly after and was there to hold his wife compassionately as she bled out. Miraculously and with quick thinking, Doc saved Beth's baby. It had been much too late to save the mother. She was able to weakly whisper something with Belle's name, but it was disjointed. It was enough though for Belle to figure out what she was struggling to say.

"U...r...ri't...shoul' 'a list'n...poss...on'n'd..."

Belle ran the broken pieces of words over and over in her mind until she could finally piece Beth's last words together. She believed Beth was trying to tell her what happened, but she couldn't be completely sure. "You're right...should have listened...poisoned..." Maybe Beth had figured the mystery out for herself. If so, it was much too late to do her any good.

Belle and Smith had only been married for less than two years, and she wasn't confident her suspicions were valid. She detested Wisteria, so she couldn't be sure what was really happening and what was only conjecture on her part. She'd tried to run it by Smith a few times, but he always shut her down. He said she was looking for cracks in the wall where there were none. He cautioned her not to meddle or cause tension in their close-knit family. She ventured to speak to Beth directly about her cousin, but Beth said Wisteria was her closest relative, and she had no reservations about her intentions.

She'd later dared to bring her concerns up one more time not too long ago. Belle tried to talk with Beth again about the food Wisteria was feeding her. Beth still insisted she trusted her cousin explicitly, so Belle was shot down once again. She should never have let it go. Now, she had to live with the deadly mistake of not telling Grey what she was thinking for the rest of her life.

It was the oddest thing no one, but Belle, ever questioned Wisteria's constant presence in the house or her constant hovering over Beth like a hen. The brothers tolerated her underfoot because Beth seemingly wanted her here. They merely avoided her as much as possible. The men worked outside or hung out in the bunkhouse with the cowboys. Grey paid Belle to do housework and cook because Beth needed the help. Belle had no choice but to try and keep the peace with this peculiar woman, but no love was ever lost between them.

Wisteria's obsessive-compulsive control forced Belle to stay quiet in the background most of the time. It raised a red flag whenever she refused to answer questions about the diet she prepared specifically for Beth when she was pregnant. Something didn't seem right about the insane interest in her cousin's health or the constant secretiveness. Belle smelled a rat, and ironically, the part Wisteria played in Beth's death would eventually be uncovered.

There was just the one-time Wisteria almost slipped up. She carried Beth's lunch tray to the kitchen and didn't clear it right away. Later, Belle ate the pudding Beth had left. It caused Belle's stomach to sour, roll, and cramp. Wisteria was livid with Belle. Soon she developed the same symptoms of indigestion as Belle. She claimed it was something contagious.

One thing was sure, Beth's baby girl couldn't be allowed

to die by Wisteria's hands. Belle would do everything possible to keep it from happening. Beth would want her infant to live.

CHAPTER 12

————— ✦ ❖ ✦ —————

Mary Ann Byrd ✦

G rey's house was beyond the scope of Mary Ann's wildest imaginations. The sight of it left her open-mouthed as she tried to make sense of it all. A huge wrap around porch beckoned her as if two arms were held wide open. Scattered rockers, swings, and straight-backed chairs sprinkled with colorful quilts and pillows made it appear a warm and friendly place. Clean glass windows sparkled like blinking eyes. Ruffled cream-colored curtains peeked through the glass from the inside. Below each window, flower boxes were attached.

"Whoa, now!" Grey called reining Mary's Pegasus to a halt. "We're here, Mary Ann Byrd. You're home."

The sound of Grey saying her new name cleared the fog in her head. She would never tire of hearing the ranger say her name. His rich voice made the syllables resonate like musical notes.

Yes, we are certainly somewhere, but this doesn't look like a place I belong.

Cowboys and a big yellow dog with a feverishly wagging

tail came forward to greet the weary travelers. Random words were exchanged amongst Grey and them all. The men offered polite nods in her direction. No doubt they'd been expecting them. Grey carefully lowered her down, but her legs buckled a bit as she touched the ground. Before she could fall, a man resembling Grey, caught her. Grey dismounted and scooped Mary Ann up in his strong, now familiar arms.

No sooner had he set her feet down on the porch, than the yellow dog braced his front legs against Mary's waist. He started sniffing, dancing, and licking her face when she went down on her knees. His tongue was wet and as wide as a paint brush. The antics made her laugh and put her and everyone else at ease. She couldn't remember hearing herself laugh before. It sounded good to her. The dog was offering unconditional love and acceptance, and she was gladly giving it back.

"This is Sunshine, Mary Ann. We call him, Sunny," Grey introduced her to his pet. "He likes you already!"

Grey and his family laughed along with her. This incident broke the uneasiness, and the tension of the moment melted away.

"I've always wanted a dog but could never have one. He's the golden-spirited hound like the one in the Greek myths!" Everyone laughed together once again, including Mary Ann herself. She'd felt the lighter weight of happiness more in the last few minutes than she'd felt it in her entire life.

"Well, you have a good dog now, Mary. Pet him, feed him, and love him. It's about all he's good for around here. If you want a puppy, you can have one of those too.

"Excuse Mary Ann and me," he apologized to his family. "We need to check on Sari first. We'll do introductions at the table later."

"Good news, finally, Grey!" exclaimed Belle. "Sari has been keeping enough of the broth down to let her rest easily! I've been giving her drops of the broth every hour since you rode out. Doc came to check on her around noon." Tears of joy rolled down the aunt's face. "She's even looking better, Grey. Doc is pleased. I'll follow you up. I can't wait to hear what you think."

Looking down at the tiny baby, Mary was enthralled. She'd never been this close to a baby before, and this one was tiny and perfect. Sari was no bigger than a small loaf of bread. The thought of her dying brought tears spilling down her cheeks. Mary wanted more than anything to hold the infant close and tell her everything was going to be all right. It was strange how her breasts dully ached. She didn't recognize this sensation.

The ranger and Sari's dear mother made this child. She is a combination of Grey and his wife. Realizing this drew Mary Ann to the baby girl. She felt no jealousy whatsoever. She'd become a part of this baby's life in her own way. Then and there she prayed and asked God to please send milk. She lightly touched the sleeping baby's soft cheek with one finger. Sari stirred but settled right back down. Her fist was no bigger than a nut.

Mary's face had become damp with silent tears. Grey was watching her closely. He put an arm around her shoulders and squeezed an encouraging hug.

"I'll try. I really will try," she whispered, looking up at him.

"I never had a doubt you wouldn't, Mary. The first time I laid my eyes on you, I knew you would help Sari."

Belle cleared her throat reminding them she was still there.

"Well, supper's waiting. I'd best get down and see it's put on the table. Come as soon as you're ready."

Grey held Mary's hand to shore up her courage as they stood in the double doorway leading into the dining room. When they were noticed, all talking ceased, and every eye was focused on the girl. She was used to stares, but these people were staring as if expecting something from her. She was struck by both shyness and fright. Her hand pulled out of Grey's grip and went to her face. She fingered a fading scar as if she'd just remembered it.

She began to fret and wondered if she could escape this attention. Her eyes cast downward as she wished to flee. It was one thing to be with Grey alone but being with his whole family was different. She dropped the hand from her face and hid it in the folds of her faded rag-tag skirt. She felt panic building and her heart thumping faster. Then her eyes found Sunny lying by the table on a worn rug. Evidently, he was trained to stay on this spot. He was good-naturedly observing her. His tongue was hanging out, and it made him look silly. The big dog's presence boosted her courage and caused her mouth to tip up on one side.

Being the gentleman he was, Grey slipped an arm around her shoulders and cleared his throat before speaking to everyone.

"This is Mary, Mary Ann Byrd. She has agreed to help me raise Sari. We got married this morning. JD performed the ceremony before we left Spur. She's my wife, Sari's ma, and your sister-in-law. This has happened suddenly for Mary and me. We all understand why it had to come about so quickly. She knows about Beth and how much I love her still, but I can find room for Mary Ann in my heart. I know each of you can too.

"Mary doesn't expect us to not mention Beth's name. It's gonna' take a long time for this family to adjust to Beth being gone. Mary Ann appreciates the nature of losses because she has been faced with struggles her whole life. Just so you know, Mary is with child. I know the complete story, and I'm choosing to stand by her and the baby. I am declaring this right here and right now.

"The past few days have been long and hard for all of us. Mary especially needs food and rest so she can nurse Sari and feel better herself. We'll give her the time and space she needs to settle in. She's not ever been part of a family before. Things we take for granted are new to her so be patient and helpful.

"Mary Anne, you now belong to this family, and they belong to you. There aren't many of us, but we're a loyal bunch. You have a strong, kind spirit, so you'll fit in with us once you get acquainted.

"These folks look scarier than they really are," he declared. There were snickers heard around the table.

"Coley here," and Coley stood, "helped you down from the horse when we arrived. He's the baby-brother, even if he is the tallest."

Smith stood next. "This is Smith. He was born after me but before Coley. He's outgrown me in size and strength.

"You've met Belle already. She and Smith are married. They've been married close to two years, so she recollects what it's like being new here and getting used to all of us. She's been taking care of Sari the past three days. She'll make you feel at home and help you in any way she can.

"Remember when I told you my sister-in-law ordered me not to come back without you? Well, she meant it. She tends to get feisty if we don't do what she says."

Chuckles showed the men were quite fond of Belle. She smiled and Mary smiled a little too. She was beginning to feel a little less anxious. She had nodded to each person but had remained speechless. She was a duck out of water around them.

Sunny, newly dubbed the golden hound, looked up from his braided rug and whined.

"Sorry, Sunshine! I didn't mean to leave you out," Grey said. He's a good dog and has the run of the house. If he follows you around too much, tell him to go to the kitchen, and he'll obey."

Sunny recognized his name and thumped his thick rope-tail loudly in agreement. He made Mary Ann laugh again just like when she first got here. His assignment would be to make her laugh often.

Grey finished by explaining Coley wasn't married, and his room was still in this house. Belle and Smith built their own home a stone's throw away. Mostly, they ate all their meals together around this table. It had belonged to their mother. The three of them were born and raised right here in this house.

Mary Ann had been stealing glimpses of the banquet of food spread across the table from one end to the other. Tempting smells permeated the room and tormented every breath she took. Her stomach was used to being empty, but she had a feeling it wouldn't take long to get used to eating regularly.

Smith came from the kitchen carrying a pottery bowl steaming with thick beef stew, chunky with vegetables, and rich with brown gravy. Belle brought in a platter of hot biscuits, and squares of yellow cornbread were already on the table. Thick, dark slices of red beets set by crisp pickle wedges. Her interest was held by the fruity preserves, creamy butter and golden honey opened and sitting on a tray.

The men already had mugs of coffee. Belle gave her a mug filled with a pleasantly fragrant hot tea sweetened with honey. After grace, everyone started talking at once, and food was passed all around. Words filled the air accompanied with laughter. Sunny had crawled silently until he was snuggled by Mary's feet and sleeping peacefully. The weight of him against the girl's leg eased her anxiety. Belle noticed Sunny and started to send him back to his rug, but Grey silently asked her to leave him.

Grey and Mary were seated by each other close enough for their bodies to touch. While Mary had been distracted, he'd been making sure both their plates were filled from the passing dishes. Seeing the full plate in front of her was surprising. She looked up at him looking down at her. He had not taken a bite of anything yet. He was generously buttering a biscuit to balance on the edge of her plate. As an afterthought he also spread it with fruit preserves and smiled at her.

Leaning so close, she could feel his warm breath on her face, Grey said, "Sweetheart, I've been telling you there's lots of food in our house. Believe me, you may have as much as you want anytime you want it. I promise, for you and our children, there will always be an abundance."

Sweetheart?

The word might as well be foreign. No one had ever called her this, no one had ever cared if she ate, or given her food before feeding themselves. She'd never been treated with any type of care. She looked down at the plate in front of her, and her stomach rumbled in anticipation of it being filled. She tucked a spoon into her stew taking just enough for a taste. After the first bite, she found it hard to hold back. She dug in like she was starving because she was starving. Grey wiped a drop of stray food from her lip with his napkin, and he was smiling at her again.

"You did really well, Mary Ann, meeting everyone just now. A full stomach should make you feel even better."

His approval pleased her, and his words warmed her. Smiling back at him, she drained the tea from her mug. It was replaced immediately with a glass of cool milk. The richness of cream coated her tongue.

Her appetite satisfied; she became interested in the table talk. Animated discussions with opinions were being volleyed all around Mary. The talk was mostly centered around livestock, fences, and the weather, especially the lack of rain. Beth's and Sari's names were mentioned. She wanted to know about the woman whose death brought her here.

Her eyes couldn't have opened any wider! A chocolate cake appeared at the end of the table. Chocolate was a flavor she'd only experienced once before. Mary recalled the richness exploding in her mouth. As Belle was serving slices, she told Mary loudly enough for the men to hear.

"Mary Ann, I'll save back two pieces for us to eat after breakfast in the morning as soon as the men head out to work."

This brought hoots of protest and teasing from the brothers. Mary's memory was not faulty. The first bite of chocolate cake met her expectations.

There were so many new things to learn on this first night in Grey's home. Who knew there was such a place as a bathing room with a tub and water piped in? Belle explained how this was possible as she filled the copper tub with warm water. It traveled through a pipe coming from a reservoir on the kitchen stove. Mary was amazed such a luxury like this was even possible.

Another person had never washed her hair before. It felt incredibly nice, and the soap Belle used smelled like lilacs. Mary kept inhaling the sweet scent deeply so she could recollect it later. It was a far cry from the harsh, lye soap she'd always used. Belle gave her the sweet-smelling bar to bathe herself after her hair was rinsed.

She left with Mary's old clothes and promised to return with fresh night clothes. In the solitude, the effects of the long day caught up with her. She yawned and fought closing her eyes. With all her heart, she wanted to stay awake long enough to see the beautiful, little baby girl again.

This time Belle let her hold Sari and offer her drops of the Indian broth. It was a wonderfully satisfying feeling to feed her and watch the little face. Mary Ann couldn't grasp exactly how it affected her, but a myriad of emotions was occurring. Grey brought her here to take care of Sari, and she wanted to do as much as possible for his daughter. She wanted so much to please him.

Belle demonstrated how to change a wet nappy cloth and how to swaddle the soft blanket around Sari to make her feel secure. To Mary's surprise, Belle left the two of them alone for several minutes. She sat quietly rocking the baby for a while. Sari smelled so clean and sweet. Mary had no prior memory to compare to the wonder of having this child in her arms. She was reluctant to leave the baby when Belle came back, but fatigue made it necessary to lie down in the bedroom next door.

Belle welcomed Mary Ann, "I'm glad you're here. God knows, we need you. He has His hand in bringing us all together. It wasn't so long-ago, God brought me to this ranch to heal. The room I fixed for you was my room. If you need anything tonight just call out. I'll be across the hall.

"Drink this cup of tea Doc prescribed and then get some rest. You look mighty worn out. Try to sleep. Grey is concerned about you. In the morning, look out your window. You'll be able to see the ranch, not all of it of course. It's a huge spread. The Byrds own a vast amount of property. I think you'll enjoy watching the animals below and the work going on around the barns. This is quite a busy place.

"Well, Mary Ann, look who's come to wish you a good night! Sunny, are you here to see your new friend? You may sleep on the rug for a while and keep her company.

"Mary, we'll make a list of things you need tomorrow. I'll send it with someone to the general store in Cap Rock to fetch them for you. I'll leave the door open a crack so Sunny can get out. Good night."

The girl barely whispered a goodnight before she slipped into sleep.

CHAPTER 13

Belle Byrd ◆

Before Smith Byrd had broken Belle from her forced servitude at the Bangtail Saloon, she'd learned a few valuable lessons about men. One was how to read them, and it had saved her more than once. Second, she'd discovered honest, dusty cowboys are worth more than dressed up dudes who are fools. Another thing, Belle could now spot a smitten cowboy from a mile away. She suspected her brother-in-law was smitten with the young girl he brought home with him.

Greyson may have married Mary Ann hastily to provide for Sari, but curiously, Belle glimpsed vague signs of something more. Belle loved Beth dearly, but it was obvious she and Grey were more like best friends They weren't infatuated with each other. The two shared a loyal, respectful, and loving relationship. They were comfortable together, but the ember of light-hearted passion was missing from their relationship.

Belle remembered falling hard for Smith. He'd returned her fervor in kind and still did. One day the big, handsome man pushed the doors open to the Bangtail Saloon and when their eyes connected, they'd both been enamored. He'd heard of a girl being held in bondage at the notorious saloon and came to see for himself if the story was true. The privation she lived under was obvious, and he risked his life to liberate Belle from the man who claimed to own her. She was being held in subservience like a slave and loaned to special customers who paid for her time.

Their subsequent love story would make a tale all its own. How desperate and alone she'd felt the day Smith came looking for her. She'd been held captive for almost a year when the gentle giant of honor came. She'd never forget how kind Smith was to a pitiful, scared saloon girl who was being forced to bear the indignities of a light skirt. He recognized she wasn't willingly participating in the debauchery. He accepted the danger and stole her out of bondage. He was her hero! She'd never forget Smith bringing her to the ranch under his protection.

Tonight, when she'd helped Mary Ann shed the tattered clothing, she'd seen evidence of the girl's mistreatment, and the ravages of constant hunger. Every bone could be traced and counted. There was little hint of the baby she carried in her belly. Belle knew what used up looked like. Thank the Lord the girl was here now where she could heal and be safe. The parties responsible for Mary's suffering would be brought to justice. Grey would see to it.

Mary Ann Barton ✦

In her exhaustion, Mary Ann's strength wilted from the soothing warmth of the bath, clean clothes, and steaming tea hitting her stomach after the big meal she'd eaten. Belle said the tea was important, so she drank it all. She would do anything to make Grey glad he'd taken a chance on her to provide Sari with milk.

Telling Sunshine he was a good dog, she snugged into the

soft bed and pulled the covers up close. The yellow hound thumped his tail in gratitude of her praise. His nearness was a comfort. Soon after Belle blew the lamp out and left, Sunny took the advantage and made his move from the rug to the end of her bed.

Greyson Byrd ◆

Grey, Belle, and Coley were awakened by piteous little cries. The noises were more like a hoarse bird than of a human baby. Before Grey could even get his pants fastened, the strange racket abruptly ceased. His heart dipped so low into his belly he forgot to breathe. In haste to reach Sari, he stubbed his big toe hard against the door frame drawing blood under the nail. He gave the sharp, throbbing pain no mind. It didn't deter him from hobbling on his heel as fast as a frightened man could move.

He reached the nursery with still unbuttoned jeans. Belle was standing in the hallway with a hand gripping the door frame for support. Her other hand was covering her mouth, and tears were streaming down her face. Grey brushed past her not even realizing Coley had shown up after him in answer to the baby's distress.

"No, no!" he groaned under his breath. Rushing ahead with tunnel vision and through the blur of panic, he was brought up short seeing the empty cradle. Slight movement in his peripheral vision drew his eyes to the rocker. Mary Ann had Sari tucked tenderly in the crook of her arm, and he could swear they were both glowing. Mary Ann was an angelic sight in a white, ruffled nightdress. Sari was greedily getting her very first taste of a mother's milk. The soft, rapid, suckling noises were the most beautiful sounds Grey had ever heard.

"Praise to God Almighty! Thank you, Jesus!" he exclaimed loudly enough to startle everyone. Grey couldn't hold back the tears of relief or keep them from slipping down his face. He didn't even try. The wonder of this moment brought the tall man literally down to his knees in front of them. He was witnessing a blessed miracle, and he knew for the first time his baby was going to make it.

Mary Ann covered her exposed breast and the baby's busy mouth with a hand. She guarded against being visible to him by arranging her clothing and the baby's blanket strategically. She was shy, but Grey had no time for modesty.

"Mary Ann, don't, please, don't. I need to see my baby nurse. I've been so afraid it was never going to happen for Sari."

Hearing the anguish in his voice and having compassion, she nodded her head and silently complied. Love, gratefulness, joy, and a host of other emotions flooded Grey's heart. He looked on Mary's face, and their eyes locked. He felt a powerful surge of something he couldn't name as he pulled the coverings back further to reveal a blushing pink breast.

For a long time, he couldn't move his eyes away from the baby's mouth. What a sight the busy little lips latched to a nipple made! It was something he'd never erase from his mind. The tiny, frothy bubbles circling Mary Ann's nipple validated the extreme measures he'd taken for his little Byrd. He laughed out loud in joy.

His eyes won the woman's gaze, and he mouthed the words. "Thank you."

She smiled freely. The beauty of this generous woman hit him like the sun on wet prairie grass. He knew right then he was falling in love with Mary Ann Byrd. Before him were his two precious girls.

Without even thinking, he brushed the baby's soft head and whispered. "Little Sari, meet your mama."

Belle and Coley had already slipped away to afford them privacy. They had backed away giving the three of time to be a family. This was a moment of tenderness between a man and a woman not to be shared with others.

CHAPTER 14

+ ❧❖❧ +

G rey had been keeping the community from learning about Mary Ann until she could acclimate to her new surroundings. This Sunday morning would be their first venture into town since Beth's tragic death. No word had preceded the family's intention to attend church today. The happy sounds of chaotic visiting, laughing, and children at play came to a halt in unison. A deafening hush fell over the crowd as conversations stopped in mid-sentences. Heads turned to take in the Byrd family's entourage. The entire congregation was taken by surprise except for Doc and the preacher who knew the family was coming.

Grey's trap led the others into the church yard and to the line of other parked conveyances. Even the rustlings of leaves and the chattering of the birds stopped as the world held its breath. Grey sensed his new wife tucking in closer behind his shoulder. He reached over discreetly and squeezed her thigh in support. He'd tried to prepare her for the strain, but he could feel her body trembling. Grey had known this would be stressful but unavoidable.

Smith and Belle were seated behind them. Coley was

following closely behind on his horse. The women were dressed in traditional black in deference to a close passing, and the men from Byrd Ranch wore the traditional black arm bands. The family sat up straight with heads high except for Mary as she did her best to stay hidden. Mary Ann fiddled nervously with the baby. Several ranch hands brought up the rear. This was a show of solidarity and a public statement of sorts.

It was inevitable Mary Ann had to come face to face with the Cap Rock Community eventually. Grey had kept news of his marriage quiet. Only Doc, the preacher, and the Byrd Ranch crew knew of her and had been sworn to secrecy. The news of his rebound would be a shock and stir a commotion, but it was time for it to be out in the open.

Grey had put off introducing his new wife and baby to the community for a couple of weeks now. The tongue wagging would be unmerciful if it wasn't tempered with the truth. He was ready to get this done before a news leak. If Mary Ann had a chance of being accepted, she had to first be acknowledged publicly by her husband and family. Grey had put a gold band on her finger this morning thwarting any question she belonged to him.

Doc and the preacher dutifully kept Sari's condition and the union to themselves. They'd helped spread the word the Byrd family wasn't accepting visitors at the ranch. Grey would encourage people to celebrate Sari's good health and introduce his wife on his own terms. Curiosity and questions were written all over the upturned faces of the parishioners. Grey stood tall facing them with his arm pulling Mary and Sari protectively close.

Most of the worshipers had already gone into the church to be seated, so the crowd outside was relatively small compared to the total number of the gathering. He could see a few women beginning to whisper and speculate under the cover of gloved hands. He knew human behavior, and nothing surprised him about the buzzard-like viciousness of people.

Grey motioned for his group to start inside together. The men nodded and tipped their hats at friends and acquaintances as they passed by but didn't stop to visit. Grey wasn't being unfriendly necessarily, but he only intended to tell this story once. The front of the church was the best place to reach everyone's ears. Whoever wasn't here, others would be more than happy to inform.

The Byrds continued walking past the seated congregation until they stood in a line at the front of the church. The ranch hands dropped off to take their seats on the back pews with hired hands from other ranches. Grey had the full attention of the audience just as he'd intended, and so he began.

"My wife died three weeks ago. She was dearly loved by all, especially her family. Many of you loved her and were loyal to her in life and no doubt, you're loyal to Beth in her death. You attended her funeral and paid your respects. Beth was a wonderful, admired woman. I love her more than my own life still. The whole family misses her presence, and we are grieving to the point of pain. We are in mourning, but Beth left a tiny baby girl behind who needed care. As it turned out, Sari was a dying baby starving to death. My daughter was dying without nourishment. I love Sari more than my own life, and I am willing to do anything my daughter needs to ensure she lives."

Many in the pews were wiping sincere tears away. He reached over and gently retrieved Sari from Mary Ann's arms and held her up so they could see her tiny pink face and rosebud lips.

"I want to present to you, Sari Elizabeth Byrd. We love her with our whole hearts and would have given everything we have to allow her to thrive. She was so tiny and weak on the day she was born. Sari lost her mother on that very day as well." Grey choked, cleared his throat, and waited a moment before continuing.

"There was nothing to feed Sari because she couldn't tolerate anything we could find. She was pale, lethargic, and losing ground rapidly with each passing hour. It was common knowledge among you we were searching for someone to nurse her. You also knew we were not having any luck.

"Doc valiantly did everything he could think of to keep her alive, but the handwriting was on the wall, and the clock couldn't be stopped."

He and the congregation looked to his friend, Doc, who nodded several times in solemn affirmation. The congregation was satisfied what Grey said was true.

"By the grace of our God Almighty, our fervent prayers were answered. We were led miraculously to this young woman who is standing by me. She was praying at the exact same time for God to help her. This is Mary Anne." He carefully placed Sari back into her arms, hoping the baby would give her the courage she needed to stand in front of these strangers. He put an arm firmly around her shoulders and pulled her closer.

"You see, Mary Ann has a baby on the way, but the father abandoned them. Being with child, Doc and Belle have been able to promote her ability to nurse Sari. She has saved Sari's life in the only way possible. She provides her life sustaining milk. No one else could do it, and because of Mary Ann, Sari is a live today. She'll grow to be a happy little girl, and one day become a beautiful woman!

"In return for Sari's life, I gladly vowed to be a pa to Mary's child and to protect them both from harm if she would be a ma to my baby. We were married lawfully before I brought her into my home, and the preacher can attest to this."

At this announcement, a few breathy gasps arose from the ladies in the crowd. Grey stopped and looked pointedly toward the preacher who also nodded and added a hearty Amen for all to see and hear. Grey pointedly surveyed the crowd. His eyes shown empty and cold when they fell upon the sour-mouthed Wisteria. She was sitting stiffly glaring at him with hellfire coming from her eyes. Her lips were pressed into a tight, thin, white line. Their eyes met as briefly as hail stones glance off of a roof. Grey broke contact first. What he saw in her eyes did not bode well. They were like two deep, darkened wells of nothingness.

"We've thrown in together to raise our children. We are a family learning to live in harmony. I am proudly introducing to you, Mary Ann Byrd. She is lawfully my wife and Sari's surrogate mama. I know this comes as a shock to ya'll, but it pleases me to live in this generous-minded community where we've always worked together for the good of each other. The Byrds have lived for three generations among you and your past kin. I know without a doubt you will accept Mary Ann and her baby as mine. I'm confident ya'll will help in every possible way to make Mary feel welcomed at every turn. God bless, ya'll."

He motioned for Smith to lead Belle to a seat. He helped Mary Ann follow with him behind her. Coley shadowed his brothers.

At dawn this morning, before church, Grey had visited Beth's grave and poured his heart out to her speaking of his love. He thanked her for leaving Sari with him to raise and assured her he'd do it right. He spoke to her again of Sari's transformational recovery. He spoke of Mary who was giving their sweet baby nourishment. He told Beth of his vow to be a father to the new baby on the way.

"Beth, we're all going to church in a minute to face the neighbors. It's got to be done, but I'm not looking forward to it, and you know it. I'd rather be beaten than to air our business. There are those who'll shun her if they don't hear this from me first. I can't allow Mary to be mistreated. She has saved Sari's life, and she's a kind and sweet person. Life has treated her badly, as bad as it gets.

"I can offer her protection. I can try every day to make up for the pain she's suffered in her life. I always will believe you approved of me going to get Mary Ann. Stumbling onto her has not been blind luck. It's been God and you working together all along.

"So, tell me, Beth, what am I to do now? Sari's alive because Mary is here and willing to care for her. I married her to make things right for Sari, but it's awful hard not to like her. It's too hard really because I'm torn up about my feelings. I don't want you to think I'm betraying you by admiring this girl. I need to honor my word to her. There's no way around the responsibilities of all it entails. The thing is, Beth, she's never known anything but rejection. She's never felt love and the support of a family in her whole life. She deserves to be loved more than anyone I've ever known.

"Mary Ann is now a part of this family. I don't need to sort it all out today. I just want you to know I'm trying to do things right. I'm seeking God's guidance and your patience with my clumsiness. Sari thriving and her health are the most important things.

"I love you, Beth Byrd. I want to do what is right by you. You were always a good wife."

A peace beyond understanding engulfed Grey like a fresh breeze. Before he stood to walk away from Beth's grave, it settled around his shoulders. He felt confident to go before the church and say the right words. He felt pardoned of the guilt he'd been struggling to shake.

Both the near and distant futures didn't frighten him anymore. Grey decided to take each day as it came, to love Sari, and to help Mary in every way possible. His love for Beth carved deep impressions into his heart, but the guilt he'd been carrying no longer felt like he couldn't be forgiven. Maybe as the time passed, the ruts would smooth out enough for him to love again. The emotions he'd been battling were too raw to deal with right now, but he was beginning to see there would be a life after Beth.

CHAPTER 15

D oc and the preacher sat around the table drinking coffee with the Byrd brothers. The happy laughing sounds of Belle and Mary Ann could be heard from the kitchen. The aroma of baked bread wafted through the doorway as two, brown crusty loaves were cooling enough to be cut. The rich, succulent smell of roast beef fresh from the oven filled the air. Belle had baked a large, white sheet cake and sealed it with pink icing early this morning before church.

This was a commemoration of the numerable reasons the Byrd household had to be thankful. The weighty position of informing people of the changes at Byrd Ranch was off Grey's shoulders. Within the walls of this house sorrow and joy were finding ways to coexist. Each had its place. It was recognition Beth's memory was still living and thankfulness Sari was alive and flourishing. It was acknowledgement Mary Ann and the baby she carried were both safe among them. Life in general was cause for celebration.

During the meal light talk of weather, cattle, and country issues were discussed as they ate. Doc elaborated on Sari's good health and toasted Mary Ann for her part in making it so. He declared it was nothing short of a miracle. No medicine known to man could have provided what Sari needed. The preacher praised God for His involvement and for the truth in Doc's words. Everyone joined in with rousing gratitude.

Grey couldn't shake the grim look on Wisteria's face this morning when he'd made his announcement. He'd feel much better if he knew what was running through the troubled woman's mind. For years she'd tried to wedge herself between Beth and himself. After the disgraceful display at Beth's funeral, he wouldn't put it past her to try and cause trouble. Grey couldn't allow her to interfere in his home again.

Just thinking about the sorceress was all it took to conjure up the devil herself! The door burst open and thudded violently against the wall, jarring pictures, dishes, and breaking a crystal vase knocked to the floor. Chaos ruled the moment. Gusts of sand, leaves, and loose vegetation blew in from outside. Sunlight backlit Wisteria, and the strong wind swirled and lifted her full skirts until the hem reached above the back of her head crowning her hair. Her dyed red locks came loose, and the metal pins holding her curls shot through the air in every direction pinging like bullets as they hit surfaces. The freed, wild wisps flew up, around, and across her face.

Cups and glasses turned over on the table spilling their contents across the white tablecloth and dripping onto the floor. Sunny stood in front of Mary Ann with fur standing up. The confusing commotion in progress was increased by a volley of loud barking and vicious sounding growls. Loose papers flew from one end of the room to the other, and some were sucked out the door. Cloth napkins were scattered on the floor. A cyclone couldn't have caused more of an uproar in the room.

All heads snapped in unison to witness the enraged

Wisteria. She was standing stiffly inside the house with her hands braced on her hips making her look bigger than she was. Black fury emanated from her eyes. The speed at which things had been torn apart temporarily had everyone in a state of mute shock. Smith had a gun drawn and zeroed in on the intruder. Coley made his way to the head of the dining room before anyone else. He managed to shut and secure the door eliminating the wind's turbulence.

Grey stood in one forceful movement, drawing, and cocking his gun. The chair legs scraped on the floor with a mighty grind preceding the chair tumbling on its back with a colossal bang as it hit the hardwood. The knotted muscles of his body pulsed with kinetic strength.

Once the realization Wisteria was alone registered on the men, guns were holstered. Grey's set expression was lethal. He was hellbent on an accounting. Wisteria's eyes had grown as big as saucers and focused solely on Grey's stare. She too was momentarily rendered speechless by the force of the uproar she'd caused.

Looking for Mary, Grey spotted her kneeling on the floor with arms thrown around Sunshine's neck in a death grip. Her face was buried out of sight in the thick fur of the dog's ruff. Trembling posture left no doubt she was terrified. The dog had stopped barking except for occasional woofs and growls thrown Wisteria's way. He was now sitting tightly against the girl. He was a barrier braced between the danger or anyone who threatened Mary.

Good boy!

Grey kept a sharp eye out for the irrational woman's next play. There was a carving knife stuck in the roast beef. He hoped it wouldn't come to making a grab for it, but if she was armed anything could happen quickly. Concern and compassion wrenched his heart for Mary Ann's fear. He wanted to relieve her of panic, but he couldn't allow himself to be distracted.

He had to stay focused on Wisteria. He shifted his eyes

slightly, briefly checking on Belle. Their gazes met but a second. It was enough to jerk his head in a barely discernable movement in the direction of Mary. He knew his sister-in-law would get to her the second tension in the room relaxed.

Smith was making his way cautiously to the front in a better position to assist Coley in subduing Wisteria if necessary. It wouldn't do to alarm her in this agitated state. The three brothers had worked together in bad situations before. They instinctively knew what to do to support each other. Doc and the preacher stood silently behind their chairs darting their eyes rapidly taking note of every element in the room. Neither were fighters, but they weren't fools either. They could be counted on to help should the need arise.

"Well, isn't this just too cozy? The happy family all breaking bread together!" Wisteria screamed in a deafening, unearthly sounding screech.

"Grey, why didn't you tell me about your little wife earlier? Were you keeping your sins under wraps? Oh, my dear, dear Beth, my poor cousin, Beth, you never deserved her. She was a saint; so sweet she was. Why she must be rolling over in her grave at how rapidly you replaced her! I swear, if it's the last thing I do, I won't let you get away with disrespecting her like this."

The preacher found his voice. "Wisteria! Stop this hysterical haranguing at once. Cease casting judgement over circumstances you know nothing about. Not one disparaging act has transpired under this roof, and your approval or disapproval isn't relevant. What had to be done has been done with my assistance and blessings. You have no idea how Grey is suffering over Beth's death, and then having to watch their baby dying a slow death right before his eyes was horrible. He did exactly what he had to do.

"God provided immediate answers to our prayers. We all listened, obeyed, and did our part. Grey orchestrated whatever arrangements had to be made to save Sari from following her mother to the grave. God gave us this special young woman from Spur. You weren't told simply because nothing here is any longer your business. The scene you've caused today is hurtful and scandalous. You're making a complete spectacle of yourself. Leave this house and these people alone immediately."

"Don't make me laugh! God, you really think God brought this stray here to save Beth's child. You are a naive idiot. The lot of you are all idiots if you think this is God's doing! It's only an excuse for Grey to get a younger and prettier woman in his bed. He took the first chance to get one."

Grey faced off with the ranting, irrational woman.

"I don't want you in my home, my life, my business, or near my family ever again. Leave! Get off this ranch. Stay away from us! I've put up with you hanging around and fawning over Beth, all these years. You've never done anything but meddle in our lives. You didn't give a fig about her or her well-being either. Beth knew it but was too kindhearted to turn you away. She preferred you keep your distance, but no, there you were, always right in the middle of our business. You were in our marriage, our home and causing endless interference. Don't pretend anymore you were only here to be helpful!

"I do have one question though before you're escorted off the property. If you genuinely cared as much as you've wanted everyone to believe, why did you mysteriously disappear the day just before Beth died? You were there in the way as always and suddenly you weren't. Not once have you bothered to inquire about the condition of Beth's baby. I find your lack of concern for her child puzzling, so answer the question. Where did you slip off to the when she became deathly ill? We all want to know."

"That baby was never supposed to live!" she screamed.

Everyone in the room gasped with opened mouths and stared at Wisteria.

She slapped a hand over her mouth, but it was too late.

She'd vomited the words out, and they couldn't be retrieved. Her eyes reflected horror at the implication of her mistake. She struggled to take command of the situation back, but it was too late once the truth was out.

Every eye was on her in stunned silence. They all waited for her to clarify or deny the declaration. Doc finally broke the silence.

"What exactly do you mean, Wisteria? Why wasn't the baby supposed to live? Do you know something I don't? What exactly happened that day before I arrived?"

"No, no, I didn't mean anything. Oh, for heaven's sake! Let's all take a step back." Wisteria chuckled and waved off her remark with a floppy hand. "This is just a ridiculous misunderstanding. Don't twist my words. I just think, well, I thought, at the time, and I still think the child would have been better off to pass with her mother. To be left motherless, the way she has been is just cruel. I meant nothing more by what I said. You're all trying to put words in my mouth."

Making things worse for herself, Wisteria continued to ramble. "Surely, Beth's weakened condition and the trauma of the difficult birth should have been enough to, well, I don't know. I never agreed with such extreme measures to be made in a last-ditch effort to, to save a baby. I meant nothing more by what I said. Don't try to read more into it. I didn't mean, oh never mind! I don't have to explain.

"All of this nonsense is water under the bridge now anyway. We've gotten off track. The real point of why I'm here, Grey, is Beth told me on the very morning of her death, specifically, to marry you should she die in childbirth. She must have had some sort of premonition because she absolutely made me promise to agree to marry you. Of course, she was so distraught, and I agreed to anything she wanted. I absolutely assured her I would do exactly as she wished.

Everyone but Mary Ann stared at her.

"Believe me, if I'd had any idea you weren't going to wait

a decent amount of time before taking another wife, I would be the one married to you right now. I would have approached you on the day of the funeral, but I assumed you'd need time to grieve, a proper amount of time.

"It's indecent you've brought in a dance hall-fevered substitute to fill your bed! Isn't it enough Smith has stooped so low?"

"Shut up!" Smith yelled.

"I can only hope I've gotten here in time to negate this farce of a marriage. Everyone will forgive you for making a bad decision in your grief. You simply made a rash move and a most outrageous mistake. It's not too late to reverse your lapse in judgement. I'll help secure an annulment. Afterall, it's common knowledge now the trash is already pregnant with a bastard!"

"Wis...ter...ia, I'm warning you to shut the fuck up, or so help me, I'll render you unable to talk!" Grey roared like a lion. "You're a bitch of a liar and always have been! Beth never told you any such thing, and we all know it. She knew how much I detest you.

"She only tolerated your continual meddling in our lives because she felt sorry for you. She hated being suffocated by you and manipulated. She didn't have it in her soul to order you to leave her house. She was too kind to run you off.

Raising his voice even louder, Grey said, "Listen to me and get this straight. Mary Ann and I are married, so you indeed are too late to interfere. Luckily for me, she agreed to marry under stressful circumstances. Sari and I are blessed to have her with us. This is Mary Ann's rightful home now! She's under my protection, and yes, her baby on the way is too. I claim her baby as mine.

"Sari needs a ma, and Mary fits the bill in every way. She'll be treated with respect by you and everyone else, or I'll have plenty to say about it! I intend to make her a good husband and care for her well. Get it through your thick skull and stay the hell clear of this ranch."

"Oh, I didn't see it! I just now get it. The baby she's carrying is yours. She is actually having your baby! No wonder you were always gone so much of the time. You've been having other women on the side. It's your baby, Grey! I just now put it together. Well, well, isn't it just too rich? I told Beth you were cheating on her all along, but she would never listen to me! You got away with it. You were cheating on her just like you cheated on me years ago with Beth. You're a cheater, Grey, a dishonorable scoundrel!"

Grey had listened to enough. "Coley, get a couple of the boys to see she gets home. Wisteria is leaving because she doesn't belong here where she's no longer allowed. I don't ever want her to set foot on this ranch again."

"You bet, Brother, sure thing! I agree, it's way past time for her to leave. I'll arrange an escort back to town."

"Grey, I must warn you. You're not going to get away with this, you two-timer, you liar. Go ahead, kick me out today, but my absence is only temporary. Mark my words, Grey Byrd, because I'll be back. You'll pay! I'll make you regret speaking to me the way you have today. This isn't over yet, not by a long shot. You'll belong to me, because you've always been meant for me from the beginning.

"I let you get away with jilting me once! Beth took you right out from under my nose, and now this sickly, diseased whore with her bastard baby has sunk her filthy claws into you. You have a lot of nerve, Grey! You'll regret how you've scorned me. I won't let it slide!"

A shadow fell over the opened doorway. Her escorts had arrived and tugged her out none too gently. The preacher followed to accompany them back to town.

The afternoon party was abruptly over, and the white cake with pink icing hadn't even been cut.

CHAPTER 16

Wisteria Winters ◆

H ell has no fury as a crazed female called out into the
open and scorned publicly. Wisteria was blinded by
rage when Grey stood before the congregation this
morning and announced what he'd done. The devil was a
deceiver and long ago had stolen Wisteria's desire to look
toward the Light. Her soul had crossed over into the deep
abyss as soon as her mother breathed her last breath. Her
heart officially seared over, and each additional murder she
got away with freely proved she was invincible.

Wisteria refused to rest until Grey's little wife along with
both babies were destroyed. Soon after, Belle would follow
them down the secret well. She'd accomplish four Byrds
killed with one stone. Wisteria had no idea what a risky game
she was playing this time. The power she believed belonged
to her was merely a dark illusion. The rug was going to be
pulled out from under her feet.

Wisteria left the ranch plotting viciously. She was being
bombarded by incoherent, irrational thoughts. She was a
human powder keg. Her psychopathic mentality rallied

against every person who'd witnessed her dressing down today. The part of her brain responsible for checks and balances wasn't operating. She'd fix them all, fix them good, and get away with it!

She paid no attention to the escorts flanking her rig as she demanded a fast-clipped pace from her poor little mare. What did they suppose she was going to do between the ranch and town? What useless buffoons! They were sent on a foolish errand. If Grey thought strong handing her off his property would keep the Byrds safe, he had a huge disappointment in store. Repercussions were following forthwith.

Her red hair flew around her head standing up in the places she'd pulled with her hands. Her clothing was wrinkled and twisted. Her eyes burned from squeezing her lids tightly shut to clear her head. When they were open her vision blurred. Her lips were in constant motion and bloody from the gnashing of her teeth.

The closer she got to town, the more she calmed and regained her wits. She was regretful of her afternoon's performance. Careless emotions had taken over this afternoon and exposed her hand prematurely. The out-of-control impression she'd projected was beneath her usual standards of conduct. Her rants were those of an insane woman. Putting too many cards on the table had her at a major disadvantage. In the heat of the confrontation, she'd recklessly slipped and cast suspicion upon herself.

The damage was done and most unfortunate, but it was fixable. She'd just have to plot her next actions carefully and move ahead faster than was prudent. Haste makes waste, but Wisteria was now forced to be swift, ruthless, and lethal. Bernard showing up unannounced in the barn a few months ago might just have been a fortuitous happenstance. He was dumber than a box of rocks, but the drunk was malleable.

For years, Bernard had received a retainer from her just for showing up once a month and keeping out of sight. In addition, money for heavy work and shutting his mouth was paid by the job. Totally off schedule one day, she'd found him in her barn. He had no intention of leaving and threatened to blackmail her if she didn't agree to hide him for as long as needed.

Wisteria had no intention of cowering under his vile demand. Slick as a whistle, the smart woman outmaneuvered him. She turned the tables by increasing his guaranteed retainer and promising a set salary for his work including food and keep. He readily agreed to this arrangement making him nothing more than her hired hand once again. What a stupid man! She was the puppet master, and he was the puppet.

Wisteria thoughtlessly pushed the buggy weight off onto the ground before she pulled back on the reins. The light vehicle stopped in motion suddenly. The tired little mare was jerked back a full step right in front of Wisteria's house. She had no intention of leading the men around back to the barn. She couldn't risk them seeing Bernard. Without looking back or speaking to the men, she headed quickly for her front door with heels clicking.

Halfway to safety, the preacher called out. "Wisteria, wait! Wait, we need to talk."

The only answer he received was a slammed door in the face. Wisteria watched covertly from the window until the men rode away. Once gone, she changed clothes and tidied her appearance before rummaging through the cabinet for a bottle of good whiskey. She hurried out the back door into the darkness. The liquor was for Bernard, and he'd do anything to have it. He went by the name BB, but she refused to call him by the ridiculous nickname. What kind of name was it for a grown man even if he was a clown?

The preacher let slip Grey's whore came from Spur, and Wisteria filed the information away as a piece of the puzzle. It was a useful coincidence since Bernard also came from Spur. There were questions needing answers, and he just might have them. Whiskey would prime him to talk more readily. The oblivious man did love his cups!

Opening the double doors just enough to step inside the barn, she pulled them shut behind her and lit the hanging lantern. "Bernard, come down. I brought you something. I thought you might be thirsty. It's Sunday, so a treat is in order. It's one of the many benefits of working for me. Come down, Bernard, you know I'm not a patient woman."

The clumsy scraping of boots on the wooden floor overhead could be heard as bits of straw and dust sifted through the cracks into her hair and falling around her feet. The disgusting man lumbered like a heavy bear down the ladder from the loft above. Once he spied the bottle she held, a gleam appeared in his eye. He knew spirits from this woman came for a price, but he was a slave to alcohol. BB would trade his right arm for one more bottle of whiskey. He had no will power when it came to alcohol. He craved the stuff, and the sorceress was adept at using his weakness against him.

"Here, let's sit on these crates while we chat together, shall we? Go ahead, open the bottle, and enjoy. You don't have to wait! Consider it a gift on the house, but I do have a few questions you may be able to answer for me. Help yourself now, go on, you can drink while we talk.

"First question is why'd you decide to come to me before you were scheduled to be back, Bernard?"

"I don't talk about it; just had me some trouble is all. It weren't none a' my fault. I'll go back one'a these days because I got me a place there. It's nuthin' to know or worry yersef 'bout, I reckon."

"You mean go back home to Spur, don't you?"

"Yep."

"Mmmmmm, I see, but why have you stayed so long?"

"I like it here," the man answered, becoming uneasy at whatever this woman might be wanting from him.

"Mmmmmm, second question, do you know a girl there

by the name of Mary Ann? She's a young girl, timid, scar on her face, thin as a rail, light brown hair, oh, and she's carrying a child?"

BB had just taken a drink and gone to swallow when the name, Mary Ann, registered on his pickled brain. He choked and spewed out what was in his mouth. While his reaction was messy and disgusting, Wisteria overlooked his lack of manners as she felt excitement building. She'd hit a cord leading to somewhere. The anticipation she felt of finding out why he was so alarmed at the mere mention of the name was exhilarating.

"Okay, obviously, you know her then, and I'm led to the next question. Who is she, Bernard?"

"Never heard of her, I just swallowed wrong, and it went down tha wrong pipe. I don't know nobody by tha' name."

"Oh, but I think you do, Bernard. Tell me her last name. I want to know who her people are. You tell me or...!"

"Cain't tell ya nothin' if I don't know nothin'!"

"Have it your way, Bernard. I'll send a telegram to Spur tomorrow and ask the territorial marshal what he knows about this girl. While I'm at it, I'll also mention where you've been keeping yourself for the last four months. Do you think he'd be interested to know your whereabouts? Wisteria laughed at his apparent distress and his suddenly pasty pallor. So, let's try this again. What is Mary Ann's last name? This is your last chance to tell me, Bernard!"

Bernard looked at the woman with hatred before he gave up the truth. "Barton, it's Barton, I guess."

Wisteria was flabbergasted almost to the point of being speechless. "Barton?" she asked loudly. "Your name's Bernard Barton, isn't it? How do you explain both of you having the same last name? What kin is she to you?"

He huffed and shook his head until his jowls snapped and flapped back and forth throwing spittle like a dog. Noisily, he downed another swig of whiskey. Then he took another before he found the courage to confess. "I'm her pa, I guess."

"Why are you guessing? Are you her pa or not?"

"It's complicated is all. A lady like you don't want to know the sordid story. It ain't a prurdy one and the tellin' of it would take too long. I never noticed ya to be a tolerant listener."

"Oh, but this is one story I'm dying to hear! I'm waiting, Bernard! Quit stalling, keep talking, and keep drinking. I've got all night, and there's more whiskey where that bottle came from. You couldn't drag me away until I hear every detail!"

Indeed, the story was complicated, and BB wasn't an articulate man. Wisteria dared not interrupt him, because his train of thought was easily lost. He'd get disoriented, and she'd have to coax him to get back on target. The liquor loosened his tongue and got him to spill the distasteful tale, but it did nothing toward keeping him focused. She was giddy by the rich treasure trove of facts she pieced together from his rambling. There was more than enough information for Wisteria to formulate a plan around. Little Miss Mary Ann was soon going to disappear!

"Bernard," Wisteria finally said sweetly, "I know you're tired and want to go to bed, but first, go around front and drive my buggy around. Take real good care of the mare, then you can retire and sleep as late as you want tomorrow."

BB was so inebriated he stumbled out into the yard under the veil of darkness. He was used to doing her bidding. Good thing he could drive the buggy, unhitch the horse, feed, and stable the animal by muscle memory alone. He'd never even remember doing those things tomorrow and probably wouldn't remember much of what he'd told the woman either.

CHAPTER 17

―◆―◖❖◗―◆―

Belle Byrd ◆

Doc made the shift from dinner guest to doctor
instinctively. Mary Ann's and her child's physical
well beings had to be assessed after Wisteria's
hysterics. It had affected everyone in the room. The tension
had been thick enough to cut with a knife. By the looks of it,
the fragile girl had been terrified by the uproar as soon as the
door burst open. The disturbing noises, insults, threats, and
accusations came before a near brawl broke out.

Removing the caustic woman from the house resulted
into quite a scene before it was over. Her fiery tirade
rendered Mary Ann pallid with signs of distress. At least
Sunny, sticking close to his new friend, had offered her a
solid source of support. Belle crawled under the table to
wrap her arms around Mary giving additional
encouragement as soon as it was safe for anyone to move.
Smith's wife with her resilient fighting spirit was
compassionate. She was always a rock when needed.

Sunshine shadowed the women up the stairs as they
exited from the dining room. Mary Ann sat on her bed as

Belle set to work pulling the curtains together to keep the light at a minimum. She helped Mary Ann to change into a soft sleeping gown and tucked her into bed with an extra quilt. Sunshine was lying on the rag rug watching. Doc produced a linen packet of medicinal tea from his bag. Belle left immediately to steep the brew in the kitchen.

She was not surprised to find the men righting things, clearing the table, clearing the mess in the dining room, and washing up the dishes. Belle smiled at them with fondness and worked amidst the gathering of activity to ready the tea. The sound of the broken glass as it was being swept into a burlap sack was a reminder of the recent pandemonium. The men were unusually quiet and subdued in contrast to their usual banter and lighthearted talk.

"How's she doing, Belle?" Grey had been waiting to find out.

With a nod of her head Bell said, "I believe she's fine, but I'm right sure you've lost your dog, Grey. Sunny refuses to leave her side. He's appointed himself as her chief protector, such a good dog!"

"If he makes her feel secure, she can claim him with my blessings. He chose her as soon as I brought her home. He grounded her with the weight of his body throughout the confusion this afternoon. Sunny attached himself to the person who needed to lean on him the most. He figured it right. It was Mary who was more frightened than anyone. I hate she had to witness the ugliness of Beth's cousin. It was a harsh attack on all of us. I saw her seething at church this morning and should have realized a storm was brewing. I'm sorry Mary had to be a witness."

"Doc's checking on things now. She seemed to be settled down, so hopefully she and the baby are both well. He seemed reassured neither had been hurt, but he was still concerned. He sent me down to prepare the tea he prescribed to help her rest. I need to get this to her. After she drinks it all, she'll sleep for a while. As soon as the doctor is satisfied,

I'm sure he'll give you a report before he leaves for town."

Belle was grateful the dining room had been restored, and the kitchen was being put in order. She thanked the men and put a fresh pot of coffee on the stove for them. She knew the three brothers had much to discuss around the kitchen table. Their talk would center around Wisteria's visit and the alarming things she'd revealed. They would each air their opinions on how to best handle the situation and keep everyone safe from threats. They'd sort through the ideas put out and together formulate a strategy.

Belle was glad Wisteria had revealed her hatred, but she also clamped her mouth shut to keep from screaming out in frustration. She'd tried to warn Smith something wasn't right. She'd told him something was off, but he wouldn't act on it without having definite proof. He was forever the peacekeeper, but this time he'd been wrong to wait.

What a day this turned out to be! She was completely drained of energy and readied herself to leave for the comfortable home she and Smith shared. Removing the cup towel covering the forgotten, special party cake, she cut three large pieces and set them with mugs of the rich, hot coffee on the table. Catching her husband's eye, she arched a brow and slightly lifted a shoulder. It wasn't to remind him she'd told him so. It was just a subtle shove in the right direction before slipping out the back door. She expected her husband to finally tell them about her suspicions.

Smith Byrd ✦

Smith caught the body language and Belle's silent message loud and clear. He knew he'd messed up and had to confess his error. He'd had a chance to give them a heads up about Wisteria, but instead had kept Belle's vague mistrust issues to himself. It was better to come clean right now and face the consequences of his misjudgment. All this time, Smith had mistakenly hoped Belle's dislike of Wisteria caused her to be biased in her opinions of the woman. He'd factored her possible prejudice into the decision not to share the sketchy theories with Grey and Coley.

His nature was to avoid confrontations and be a peacemaker. Being passive may have allowed a deadly family catastrophe. The sudden death of his sister-in-law followed by Wisteria's scene today lined up with his wife's observations. Since Beth passed, he'd thought a lot about the things Belle had told him. Still there was no absolute proof to back the allegations. He was sorry he had not given his brothers the right to make up their own minds.

"Boys, I need to unburden my conscience. You deserve to know what Belle said. She's been suspicious of Wisteria's actions for a while, and I've kept her words to myself. She tried to get me to listen, but I couldn't fathom her accusations as being correct," Smith sighed.

"Everything my wife said started with the words, I think, I suspect, maybe, could have, or might have been. Belle only had notions but no clues. The two women plainly don't like each other, and I didn't take it seriously like I should have. I thought Belle was just seeing things she wanted to see.

"There was never anything definite to prove to me Wisteria was causing Beth to be sick," Smith said. "Belle's been telling me of strange behaviors and possible deceitfulness for months. It could be Beth's cousin has been up to no good and very clever at covering her tracks. If Wisteria's guilty, she's been careful not to leave a trace of real evidence to show for it.

"Belle's resentful of how catty, hateful and disrespectful Wisteria treats her. She's sweet as syrup in front of people, but she's completely rude and bossy the rest of the time. She's demeaning and acts like Belle is a house servant.

"I love Belle. I did listen to what she was saying, but I thought she just had hurt feelings. I found it hard to believe it was anything more than two women not getting along. What Belle thought she was seeing sounded crazy. I turned a blind eye and deaf ear to it and hoped it would all blow over. I dismissed it, and now I regret it."

Here, Coley offered backup support. "I could feel the tension in this house. Wisteria was mean, impatient, critical, and treated Belle like an outsider when you weren't here, Grey. I saw Belle ignoring her too, giving Wisteria the cold shoulder, answering her with single words, and making no eye contact. I also chalked it up to women not getting along. Smith, I understand you thinking the problem could be accounted to women fighting.

"When you were home, Grey, Wisteria didn't poke the bear, and she left Belle alone. Every time you came home after completing your work on a Ranger assignment, Wisteria always left to take care of business in Cap Rock. You never saw what we were witnessing. If Smith did wrong not to say something to you about the situation here, then I guess I'm just as guilty."

Grey gave a low, guttural groan expressing his own distress. "You're right, Coley, I was gone and wasn't taking care of my own household. I've been too busy helping other people with their problems to take care of my family. I'm the one to blame. The truth is I have used being a Texas Ranger as an excuse to stay away from the ranch because I can't stand Wisteria and never could. I didn't keep it a secret from her or Beth either. So yes, I was aware Wisteria tried to stay out of my way.

"I'm struggling with my share of guilt. I was wrong for being away so much of the time. The things I've let happen in my home to Beth and Belle are totally unacceptable. Now, Mary Ann is on her shit list, and Sari will be affected if Wisteria starts hanging around again. I can't let Wisteria continue to do more damage to my family.

"Nothing is the fault of either of you, but Smith, you and Coley should've called me out on my neglect. I wish you'd jumped my ass! What's behind us is water gone under the bridge, gallons and gallons of it, but there will be changes on from here on out. I'm gonna make it different where Sari and Mary Ann are concerned. I'm turning in my badge as soon as I find the men responsible for hurting Mary. When it's settled, I won't ride for the Rangers anymore. I'm staying close to the ranch.

"I promised Beth on her grave I won't be making the same mistakes again in this life. Sari's alive, and I've been given a second chance with another good woman. It's either all in or all out this time around, and my mind is made up for me to be all.

"Smith, apologize to your wife and make amends. We never know how much more time we've got left with a person we love. Belle is a good woman, and we're lucky to have her in this family. I wish I could make things right with Beth. I wasn't a good husband because I only provided for my wife and gave her a house to live in. I'll die being forever sorry for it, for neglecting Beth. For the rest of my days, I'll have to live with what I've done. I swear I'll take much better care of my daughter and Mary Ann."

CHAPTER 18

S mith sighed with relief to finally be unburdening his conscience. "The afternoon I heard Beth passed, the news hit me like a ton of rocks. All the past grievances Belle had mentioned started repeating over-and-over in my head. I berated myself for dismissing Belle's observations. Now, I regret not having brought them to you and Coley. Grey, I should have given you the chance to hear Belle for yourself and then maybe Beth would still be here. I'll carry the cost of my stubbornness around with me forever. If the unthinkable is true, it's not too late to protect Mary Ann, Sari, and Belle from danger."

"Smith, tell us your recollections of everything Belle said to you. We'll start with what she was seeing and try to make some sense of it. If there are enough pieces pointing toward Wisteria's guilt, we'll put our heads together and figure out how to proceed from here," said Grey.

"Belle resented Wisteria constantly being under foot and behaving like the house manager. Coley and I had even talked about how she'd taken over. In truth, we did our best to stay away from being indoors, but Belle had to work inside every day. She was trapped under Wisteria's high and mighty demands.

"Belle learned years ago how to silently blend into the walls, so she's good at going unnoticed. If she heard Wisteria coming, she'd slip out another way if possible. She kept a close eye on her movements around the house and anticipated where Wisteria would be next.

"Belle feels convinced Wisteria only pretended loyal dedication to Beth and was actually indifferent to her best interests. She sensed Wisteria planned every situation to keep family and friends separated from her. Beth confided she'd grown weary of her cousin's controlling presence, because she said as much to Belle one day. She told her she felt immensely sorry her first cousin didn't have a family of her own. She said it was her obligation to make a place for Wisteria here on the ranch because she felt pity for her. We all know from experience Beth was good to a fault, kindhearted, and self-sacrificing to anyone she thought needed her help.

"Belle has enjoyed working here, Grey except for Wisteria's annoying interference. She's liked earning her own pocket money, but she would have helped Beth even without the sum you pay her. She loved assisting Beth, keeping house, cooking, and doing general chores. They got along like two giggling schoolgirls when Wisteria wasn't around. Beth taught Belle everything about maintaining a functional home, and they worked right beside each other when Belle wasn't in bed with one of her sick spells.

"When Wisteria was away from the ranch taking care of her business interests, Beth was heartier and took great delight in keeping house, visiting friends, and being charitable in the community. The two sister-friends talked and laughed together throughout their days alone. The whole atmosphere of this house was relaxed and pleasant without Wisteria's influence. Those were Beth's best times."

Smith shook his head and stroked his chin for a moment

as if remembering how the sisters-in-law were together. He knew his wife loved Beth.

Then, Smith continued. "Belle said usually not long after Wisteria would arrive back on the ranch from one of her business trips, Beth would have a relapse. She'd get weak, sick, and end up in bed all over again. Belle wondered on more than one occasion if the timing was more than coincidence. She finally broached the possibility with Beth, but she'd have no part of the idea. Belle only brought it up to her one other time, and Beth still wouldn't consider it.

"Wisteria took on the sole role of being Beth's nursemaid and hovered over her bedside constantly. She'd be here for days on end and insisted on preparing special trays of food for Beth to eat alone in her room. Every bite and every sip she put into her mouth came from Wisteria personally.

"She was continually combining and mixing herbs she referred to as natural medicine the way God intended. She said she was trying to give Beth relief from the uncomfortable bouts of vapors and headaches. Wisteria was secretive, and Belle wasn't even allowed in Beth's room to clean or pick up the trays and leftovers. In fact, Wisteria avoided letting her even see or talk to Beth unsupervised. She told her to stay out of the darkened bedroom entirely and guarded against her disturbing her sister-in-law in any way.

"Once, Beth's lunch tray was forgotten on the kitchen counter, and Belle ate some of the pudding which hadn't been touched. She started having stomach cramps and became vaguely ill shortly after. When she mentioned it, Wisteria became livid, and her overreaction seemed unnecessary to Belle. Low and behold, Wisteria started having the same symptoms. It entered Belle's mind after Wisteria sent her home for the rest of the day. Wisteria used her similar sickness to dismiss the whole incident as a contagious stomach ailment.

"Another time, a lunch tray was left in the kitchen, and Belle finally scraped the leftovers into the cat's dish on the back porch. When Wisteria realized she'd neglected to clean the tray herself, she wanted to know what Belle had done with the leftovers. She demanded the scraps of food be retrieved and thrown in the trash. To keep the peace, Belle went out to collect them, but it was too late. The cat had already licked the bowl clean. The next morning, it was lying dead under the porch, and Wisteria apparently buried it herself, because it disappeared. This was strange behavior for a woman who expected to be waited on hand and foot."

Coley let out a noisy breathed. "Good, Lord! I remember that striped tomcat dying but didn't know anything about the story you just told. He was the best mouser we had around here, so I took notice when he died under the porch. He had looked healthy enough to me and then for no reason he was dead. I thought it was possible a snake had bitten him, but when I went to examine the carcass later, it was already gone. I just figured one of the hands had buried it, so I got busy with something else and forgot. Never did it enter my mind Wisteria was the one who'd buried the cat."

Smith continued. "Unless it's working with animals, I don't know much about childbirth, but Belle thought it questionable when Beth suddenly lost the third baby she carried before Sari. She had been feeling well and was supervising the canning season every day. Then Wisteria showed up after more than a couple of weeks of being gone, and by the next morning Beth had started cramping and spotting. She lost the baby soon after, and as usual, Wisteria privately nursed her through the delivery and her recuperation.

"Evidently, she left the house unnoticed with the contents of the birthing pan because the fluids mysteriously went missing before Doc got here. When he found out the afterbirth was gone, Doc was madder than a wet hen because he hadn't inspected it for himself. He said it needed to be checked for tears in the birth sack and to make sure everything had been entirely expelled. He was furious about a careless oversight so important and reminded Wisteria she'd assisted him in too many births to forget his procedures. Belle overheard him dressing her down.

"Belle thought Wisteria acted differently whenever you came home, Grey. She'd put her best foot forward, actin' all friendly and sweet-like. She'd be a real charmer until you and Beth slipped into the bedroom behind your closed door. Then she'd turn on Belle, agitated, snippy, mean, and couldn't leave the ranch fast enough.

"Belle walked into your bedroom to put something away." Smith's eyes grew bigger with what he'd say next. "She swore Wisteria was standing in front of the opened wardrobe. The peculiar woman was sniffing your things, Grey! Her head was completely in the hollow of the cabinet. She got riled when she turned around and noticed Belle standing in the doorway, watching without making a sound. She slammed the wardrobe shut and huffed out of the room." This disturbing recount brought audible reactions from both Grey and Coley. Smith wrinkled his nose up, looking to the ceiling recalling his own initial revulsion.

Smith adding his own conclusion after recalling and putting together all of Belle's misgivings was thinking Wisteria might really be a threat. "Grey if Belle's on the right track, Wisteria most likely caused all three of the babies before Sari to die. How Sari slipped by her, God only knows! I keep thinking about Wisteria saying Sari should have died."

Grey was thoughtful for a minute. "I've been speculating on the meaning of Wisteria's words and misplaced anger today. Nothing you've just told surprises me. In the past I've seen and heard things not setting well with me. I let them all ride, pretending it wasn't my responsibility to sort them out if Beth was willing to tolerate her cousin. I depended on Beth to keep her meddlesome relative in check. Now I realize this has been too much for Beth to handle alone. I'm the one in the wrong here, Smith, not you. I've willingly turned a blind eye to what was happening under my own roof.

"There are many things for the three of us to be concerned about after her unkind and false accusations against you, Belle, Mary Ann, Sari, and me." He let out a long, tired sigh. "She's shown her hand, and we're all in her sights. Belle, especially, is too close to her secrets. She's been the only one of us to hinder Wisteria's movements in any way. Her watchful eyes have made things more complicated for Wisteria to stay out of the light.

"Smith, you better keep a close watch on Belle. Post a man to hang around the house during the day and to walk her to and from your place. Don't let her off this ranch without an escort either.

"I was aware Beth was tiring of Wisteria's presence here in the house. In fact, looking back, she didn't really want her around anymore. She told me a few objections she had against her. I advised Beth to send her cousin packing, and I should have taken care of it myself. I'm guilty. I was Beth's husband, and I should have protected my wife."

Coley spoke up. "The immediate problem, and the only one we have any control over is how to keep Wisteria away from this ranch and away from Sari and the women. They're all in danger from what I've heard. The mayhem Wisteria caused this afternoon is a serious wake-up call. We've got to be prepared for repercussions. Wisteria is a loose cannon. I'm not sure how we missed this for so long. We can't afford to make more mistakes."

Backing up Coley, and agreeing with both brothers, Grey supported their theories. "I'm thinking the same way, boys. Losing the three babies and Beth's death may not have happened without criminal assistance. Evidence is stacking up against Wisteria. If we're right, she's gotten a taste for killing and will likely strike again. We can't assume she's finished. Serialized killers never are."

"Coley, you're good at investigation. How would you feel about doing some detective work?" Grey asked him.

"I'm ready to roll, big brother, anytime. Tell me where to start and what I'm looking to find. I'm ready for whatever you want, Grey."

"Tomorrow morning, I suggest you take Wisteria's upstairs room apart systematically. Go through it with a fine-toothed comb. Look for loose floorboards, baseboards, and anyplace something could be hidden. While you're at it, you might as well go ahead and bundle up anything belonging to her because she's not coming back into this house. After you're done, go talk to Doc and let him know our suspicions. Find out if he has any doubts himself about Beth's death or Wisteria's behavior. Also, talk to him about herbs and poisons. Then take Wisteria's belongings to her as an excuse to make an innocent contact with her. Get a feel for her place so later, you can search around it easier. When she's not there, systematically check it all out for clues or anything peculiar. This will keep you busy for a while.

"I'm anxious to talk with Belle myself and ask her some specific questions. I'll caution Mary Ann to keep herself and the baby close to the house until I say it's okay to move around freely again. I won't reveal much to her, but she's bound to suspect something is up. We all need to keep keener eyes on around here.

"I'll contact my captain and tell him the situation. It couldn't hurt to have a ranger stationed undercover in town to listen for information on Wisteria's dealings. It would be helpful to have another set of eyes and ears quietly looking around, listening, and keeping track of Wisteria's movements. Somebody in town may know something. Walls do have ears too, and sooner or later, every criminal messes up, like Wisteria did today.

"Smith, tell the men to keep alert for signs of trouble. Every person needs to be on the lookout for anyone hanging around or anything out of the ordinary. Make sure everyone stays armed until further notice. Tighten security up around here day and night."

CHAPTER 19

Greyson Byrd ✦

G rey sat alone in deep thought until long after his brothers left, and the sun had gone down. He needed to do something soon to reassure Mary Ann she was secure and to tighten the connection between them. There were no doubts in his mind about desiring a relationship with his wife. He just wasn't completely sure when he wanted it or what he wanted it to resemble.

Dire circumstances made it necessary for them to marry on the heels of Beth's death. Their union had complex hurdles to jump from the beginning, but the day he brought his new wife to Byrd Ranch, he was committed to making the best of it. Learning the lesson, the hard way, he now understood a woman required more than food, clothing, and a roof over her head. Those were the easy things to supply. Keeping a woman safe and cultivating feelings of trust and affection would take a great deal more effort.

What a precious gift she was to his daughter and him! It could only have been God Who brought them together with the glue of their two children. He had to make Mary Ann believe he could see her beauty, her good heart, and would be sensitive to her vulnerability. If he could only make her believe he was trustworthy, he could slowly start building the awareness of worth she'd be able to find in herself. Grey had promised her to take the intimacies of marriage slowly, but he'd also pledged they'd figure it out together as they went along.

Physical and emotional marks put upon her by contemptible men had caused damage. Physical marks were evidence she was a fighter and a survivor, but emotional marks were different. They scratched more than just the surface of a person. The destruction of emotional pain ran deeper and was invisible. These tracks made her question her own value. Bullies, cowards, poverty, and the lack of love had stolen her self-confidence. Her pa had caused his own child to suffer these indignities. His final insult had been to throw her to the dogs. Grey had no use for scum like BB Barton.

In the beginning, Grey thought it prudent to keep a distance between the girl and himself until after her baby was born. It seemed a reasonable plan, but now he wasn't so sure it was the right plan. After she'd been assaulted by the terrible words hurled at her this afternoon, she must need to be engulfed in support and to learn she had a husband for protection. She needed to realize she'd found a forever place with him. He wanted her to absolutely feel safe.

She had never experienced living with people and being a part of a family. It was overwhelming and would take getting familiar with everyone. Mary Ann needed to learn to rely upon the people here. With time and patience, he would work to be her guide. Proving he was truly and sincerely hers would take time and actions, but for now, a personal connection with him needed to be made. It had to be more than just words. He wasn't sure where this first step would lead, but he knew she needed to feel loved.

Both were badly broken to pieces by life. A big effort

toward piecing the jagged shards of their lives back together and filling the cracks was necessary. A sudden urgency to go to Mary Ann swelled within him. He yearned to shore up her strength and courage as well as regain some of his own starch. The baby's cry and a mother's answering footsteps were the catalysts triggering him into action.

He sailed the stairs taking two at a time until he reached the top. He stopped on hearing Mary softly humming a melody and the rhythmic creaking of the rocking chair's dry joints. Without a sound he continued to the door of the nursery and stood there perfectly still watching his baby receiving the life-sustaining nourishment. What a glorious, private, and profound moment to witness! He'd never tire of seeing a mother with a child. His personal grieving period and never-ending loyalty to Beth were real, but seeing the multiplicity of the picture before him, was reality.

The baby's mouth unlatched with a barely audible pop, and Mary kissed the top of her head. She raised the babe gently to her chest stroking Sari's little back until a soft, blow of air escaped. She kissed the tiny sweetheart once again and tenderly swaddled the infant. After carefully placing the small bundle into the cradle, she laid her hand on Sari's fuzzy head and sighed with satisfaction as only a mother would. It occurred to him Sari never had to know the misfortune of being motherless because of this unselfish woman.

Mary Ann turned toward the door without looking up and made to straighten the top of her gown refastening the buttons but not before Grey looked his fill of the contour of a lovely breast. The nipple was still swollen, distended, wet, and darkened in color. Without looking up she moved to leave the nursery, but instead, she bumped into the solid wall of a man in the doorway. She gasped and looked up with surprise into Grey's face.

The smile Grey had as he looked down into Mary Ann's eyes eased the brief embarrassment she felt, but it was soon replaced with something else. He chuckled and reached out to steady her with big, gentle hands. He sorely had to tame the urge to pull her into his arms after what he'd just witnessed. Prudently, he retreated a step allowing her to pass but not without brushing against him.

Mary Ann was surprised when she heard his steps following her in into the bedroom. The door latch clicked behind them, and they were shut in the bedroom together. Alarmed and confused she stood waiting, hardly daring to breathe. The small space between them was thick with tension. She held her position, and he inhaled the scent of lilacs lingering from the soap she'd used to bathe.

"Mary Ann, my sweet girl, we should talk. We need to talk. I've purposely given you time to get settled into your new home. Everything must seem so different to you here. Lots of new experiences are bombarding you from every direction, but I want you to feel this is your house you share with Sari and me.

"The differences and changes you've made in Sari are miraculous. I can hardly see the tiny, starving baby she was before you took her to mother. She's gaining weight, filling out, and no longer sounds like a croaky, wounded chick. Doc is incredibly pleased with her progress and with yours. It's hard not to notice your rosy cheeks along with your womanly curves making their appearances. I'm glad to see you eating and resting, and to see the smile you so often have on your lips now is exciting.

"Belle loves having you here with her in the daytime. I've noticed she's making sure you have nice clothes and things ladies like. I heartily approve of anything making you happy. If you need or want for anything else, anything at all, tell me. You have no idea how happy I am to have you here. Are you doing as well as you seem, Mary Ann?"

"How could I not be satisfied with so much to eat and milk to drink? I've never seen so much available food. There's no end to it, and I have a room of my own, a warm, soft bed, and so many nice people. I even have a dog to visit me. Yes, to your question, I'm more than comfortable here.

"The baby, oh, how I love Sari! She smells so good and sweet. When I hold her in my arms, she fills me with love inside. I've never known what it's like to feel love until now. Growing up happiness was so far away and unreachable. I've never felt so excited and full of hope. Thank you, for finding me, Grey."

"Everything I have belongs to you, Mary Ann. You've finally found your forever home. Relax, let your guard down because you're here with me. You've always deserved to be happy and loved Mary. You belong to me, now. I want to keep you safe and sound. I'm your husband, you're my wife, and Sari's your little girl. Together we make our own small family. What would have happened to Sari if you hadn't agreed to marry me? It's hard to even consider the consequences. She wouldn't be alive tonight, because you are the one responsible for pulling her back from a sure death. I credit you for her life. Soon, we'll be adding another baby, and then we'll be four. Don't think I've forgotten the baby who will soon be joining us.

"There was an unpleasant commotion today, Mary Ann, and I want to apologize for the scare it caused you. It was stressful for all of us, and you must have many thoughts and questions running through your mind. I've been replaying what happened over and over myself. Beth's cousin, Wisteria, barging in on us has brought up many concerns.

"You don't need to be afraid, because my brothers and I are taking steps to keep everyone safe from it ever happening again. You'll notice outside doors being locked more often, men outside guarding the house, and other new security precautions. Mary, I want you, Belle, and Sari sticking closer to the house. You may sit on the porches, but don't venture farther than the yard until I say otherwise. There will be no more afternoon walks unless someone is with you."

Grey was still standing at Mary Ann's back with his

hands holding possessively to her upper arms. He had affectionately pulled her shoulders back until she was leaning against him. They were so close their bodies were radiating a common heat. His work callused hands caught here and there on the thin, white cotton of her gown. At first, he'd felt her brace slightly against his familiarity, but she soon surrendered to him and relaxed, allowing him to support her.

Masculine awareness shot through him. It was like the feeling he'd had the moment she'd opened the door to JD. He'd gotten his first look at her then, and she was beautiful. She'd held herself so bravely and had a determined presence in her countenance. Her stance solicited no pity. He only knew what JD had told him, and yet, he remembered her as recognizable from his friend's description alone. He could see her completely, and his heart called out to her as he stood on the old porch. He knew he wanted her then, and he was certain they could help each other.

Right now, he felt the very same yearning Mary evoked when he'd handfed her the juicy, red apple one slice at a time on the way home. He'd watched entranced as she examined the fruit in awe, smelling of it, and wanting to share it with him. He was mesmerized as her pink tongue darted out to catch the errant drop of sweet juice. It was so apparent she wouldn't let even a tiny taste go to waste. She was so hungry and waited in apt anticipation for each sliver of the fruit's creamy flesh. She had clearly savored every bite. Her greediness brought on by need drove him crazy.

Grey would never forget what seeing this small slip of a girl nursing his daughter for the first time did to him. He couldn't take his eyes off Sari's teeny, rosebud lips latched to Mary's nipple. Her little cheeks flexed with every suckle. The milk frothed and collected around the skin-to-skin connection bringing him to tears. The little mama and her baby, the two angels, belonged to him. They were an endowment of ultimate worth.

He would not make excuses or give explanations to anyone questioning his marrying so abruptly after Beth's passing. He was proud of this girl and Beth's baby. He was lucky Mary had agreed to join herself to him and raise his child as her own. He would honor his word and move forward slowly, but the resolve of keeping his distance from his wife much longer was weakening. She required his closeness just as Sari required her milk. Mary was starved for care, right now, in the present, and Lord help him, he wanted her comfort too.

Instinctively this afternoon when all hell broke loose, he'd been charged with a fierce desire to shield her from Wisteria's fury and cruel words. Grey knew then how hard he'd fight to do whatever it took to keep both his girls protected.

"Mary Ann, please don't be frightened of me, because hurting you would be the end of me. I'll never raise a hand to you. I'll never approach you in anger. You and Sari are my treasures. I will destroy anyone who threatens your wellbeing. You are secure here with me, and I'll protect you with everything in my power.

"You and I are tied together, sweet girl. I am bound to you as your husband, and you are bound to me as my wife. We will let nothing come between us and our vows to each other. Nothing we've faced before this moment, or anything coming after, will tear us asunder.

"Sit on the bed with me. Will you, please?"

She obliged him, and he took a seat by her. Grey cupped her face in his hands and gently turned her to meet his eyes. The hints of emotion he saw playing on her face gave him hope. The tip of her pink tongue slipped out nervously to wet her bottom lip. It was his undoing. Moving one hand to the back of her neck and with the other still on a cheek, he tilted her head back and lowered his lips to brush softly against hers. Mary Ann did not shy away from his advances, nor did she reciprocate. Encouraged though, he searched her expression and dared to kiss her again. He applied enough pressure this time, so she knew she'd been kissed.

Grey had no intention of pushing his luck. He pulled back and smiled at her.

"I've never been kissed before, Grey. It felt nice. I didn't know what it might be like, but I enjoyed it."

Grey nodded, understanding her lack of experience.

"Mary Ann, you're the pluckiest woman I've ever known, a fighter, a survivor. The difficulties and unmerited pain you've had to endure would have broken most women. Yet your spirit has stayed intact through it all. You're amazing, Mary. I'm proud to call you, my wife. I am humbled because you do me a great honor in carrying my name.

"When I think of what you've suffered at the hands of no-accounts, I want to track them all down, including your pa. You are innocent of what's been done to you by him and the filthy outlaws. They'll each pay the price equivalent to their crimes. I won't rest until all debts are collected. I'll make sure justice is meted out to anyone who's touched you before me. The visible scars are the least of the harm, I'm thinking. Scars, seen or unseen, will not come between us. One day soon, I'll look at every inch of you, and then you'll know I only see Mary Ann Byrd. They've scarred you in so many ways, but you've not been spoiled for me, Sweetheart.

"It's a powerful thing to be the first man who has ever kissed your lips and to know you liked my attention. There's so much more for us to explore in marriage but all-in good time when we're both ready. Until then, you should know I'm going to kiss you every day from now until my last breath. Our caresses will just keep getting better and better."

Tears slipped down her reddened and heated skin. Holding her cheeks in his hands, he caught the wetness with his thumbs and placed another kiss on her plump lips. Much to his joy, he felt the moment she surrendered by the relaxing of her muscles. Her virginal trust and submission flooded him with a potent lust. His manhood stiffened as she offered herself to be adored.

He'd not considered the sensual affect her initial acceptance of him might have. It flooded him with pleasurable sensations, giving him a great deal to look toward. It filled his heart with the stirrings of passion. He would allow his Mary all the time she needed. He would court and coax her until she fell in love with him.

CHAPTER 20

G rey laid his big hands upon Mary's smaller ones and encouragingly squeezed. She looked up into his face, and he heard the slightest hitch in her breathing.

"Mary Ann, may I put my hands on the swell of your stomach? I'll only touch with your permission. Please, may I? The life growing there is also mine to love and raise with you. I need to feel a bond with this baby. I will teach him to ride, ranch, obey the law and know how to treat women with all due respect. I have claimed him as my own. He's our baby, yours and mine, Mary Ann."

"Wait, him, you said? You think this baby is a boy?" She asked in such a soft whisper, he could barely make out the words.

"Could be, why not? No one can know for sure. It's just as likely to be a girl, and she'll be as smart, brave, gentle, and pretty as her mama. I'll be just as happy with either, a boy or a girl. I haven't known you very long, Mary, but long enough to see those qualities in you. I know your gentleness is not a weakness. You're the exact opposite of weak woman.

"You are the strongest female I've ever met. You've lived through miserable circumstances using only your wit and determination. It takes a special person to do what you have done. I admire you, Mary."

They genuinely smiled at each other. She nodded her head slightly giving consent for Grey to lay his hands on her belly.

"Stand up and face me, Sweetheart. I'll stay seated here on the bed. Step closer so my arms can easily reach you. They chuckled nervously together like two people sharing a secret. With great care and respect, he gently touched her. His big, calloused hands covered the firm rounded tummy. The mound held the beginning of a new life. As if in greeting, the baby quickened. He eagerly bent forward and put his ear where he'd felt the flutter. The baby didn't move again, but he thought he could hear his heartbeat. He stayed there for a minute.

Slowly, his eyes took her in from head to toe and back. Without thinking, he stood and drew her to himself. She was encased and warm in his arms. Grey kissed the top of her head, her eyelids, and trailed light kisses down the length of her neck. Releasing her, his hands moved to Mary's face tilting it so their lips could meet. He rubbed his against her softer ones. She did not pull away, so he deepened the kiss. Again, she stayed in place. He wouldn't go any farther tonight. It was plenty of getting acquainted for now. Hopefully, it was enough to help her forget about the trouble with Wisteria.

"Mary, let me tuck you into bed. You need to sleep. Sari will be wanting you again before you know it. I'll check on her before I head to bed. Have sweet dreams, Darlin'."

By the time he closed the door to leave, she had closed her eyes and shut out the world. Grey returned to the kitchen table, alone again and in the dark. His mind was still focused on Wisteria's unwelcomed visit to the ranch and what it all meant. It led to his brothers and himself to suspect her of murdering Beth. If they were correct, she posed a hazard for everyone in the family. There was no way he'd sleep tonight.

He also kept reliving how sweetly Mary Ann responded to his advances. Their first kisses tasted good, and his arms wrapped around her felt right. Grey couldn't get over feeling the baby quicken. Hearing his heartbeat touched him. It had been nice to experience this with Mary. He'd treat the boy, or girl, like his own blood. He secretly hoped it might be a boy.

He sipped warmed-over coffee, long ago gone tepid, while he worried over the problem Wisteria presented. If he had his way, she'd be corralled and awaiting trial in a jail cell soon. No doubt she'd hire the best lawyer in Texas to get her off. If they could get evidence proving her guilt beyond a shadow of doubt, it wouldn't matter how much she paid for a fancy city lawyer.

Grey looked forward to watching her hang by the neck and swinging. He'd even volunteer to pull the lever dropping her to her death. His dear Beth would have her own justice. One way or another, he and his brothers would uncover enough evidence to prove the bitch murdered Beth along with the first three babies she'd tried to carry. Right now, Beth's cousin posed the most immediate threat to his family. Getting her locked up had to be his priority. Then he would start tracking Mary's tormentors.

Tomorrow, Coley would tear her room at the ranch apart, board-by-board if necessary. She must have left something incriminating behind. Coley had a knack for undercover investigating. Grey had used him before on cases. He would scour every nook and cranny of her house and property in town. It would be a triumphant day when enough was found to issue a warrant for her arrest.

The pounding on the front door was going to wake the whole house. Who could it be at this hour? Greyson hurried to answer.

"Stop! Just give me a minute, will ya'?"

Throwing the door open, Grey discovered JD standing on his front porch!

"JD, you son of a gun! It's always good to see you, but do we have to keep meeting in the middle of the night? Come in, come in, I'll offer you a cup of reheated coffee and a piece of the party cake Belle baked."

"Sounds good, and I won't turn either one down! This late hour wasn't of my choosing, Grey, but looks like you've not been to bed yourself. You're still dressed! What's keeping you from sleeping? What's happening here? Is the baby, okay?"

"No, I mean, yes! Sari couldn't be doing any better. She's out of the woods, thanks to Mary Ann."

"How are you and Mary getting along together? I've been wondering, but I knew you'd see to it she's all right."

Grey's face softened, and his smile told all JD needed to know. He had the look of a contented man.

"Mary Ann is well. She's putting on some weight, getting lots of rest, and taking to being a mother like a professional. I'm truly pleased with her progress. She's interacting with the family more and finding her own place to fit in. She's adjusting to her new life. If I'm not mistaken, she gets a little happier every day. You'll see it for yourself.

"Sunday was an unsettling day for all of us though. We've been left on edge. It turned out to be one of those days gone off the rails. Sunset left us with a lot on our minds. It's the reason I can't sleep, but let's forget about my worries.

"Why are ya' sitting at my kitchen table and getting ready to eat cake and drink leftover coffee at this awful hour? What's so important it brought you all the way to Byrd Ranch? It must be urgent, or you'd be tucked away in a warm bed. Who're you after this time?"

Grey had the oil lamp lit in the middle of the table. The shadows cast on the surrounding walls were dark silhouettes. He brought over another cup and the coffee pot keeping warm on the woodstove. He poured the cup full for his friend and refilled his own. When he returned to the stove, he threw in a couple of wood chunks to help take the chill out of the night air. He returned to the table with forks and two saucers of cake.

JD couldn't wait any longer to give Grey the news. "Grey, got a definite lead on locating the men who hurt Mary. There's no time to waste. A few hours ago, a posse left to go after 'em. Several lawmen are riding along. I plan on joining up with them at a rendezvous point. I knew you'd want to be in on this.

"I can't get what happened to Mary Ann out of my mind. Nothing can make it better except bringing them to meet their ends. Surely, you want the chance to be there when they're caught?" JD cocked an eye and lowered his chin at Grey as if it was a rhetorical question."

"Hell, yeah! Thinking of how right ropes looped around their sorry necks would look is constantly on my mind. I won't be satisfied until I see them six feet under and no longer able to hurt Mary or any other woman. I intend to see BB Barton pay his dues too. Do you think he'll be riding with them?"

"Could be, but I doubt it. I don't figure him as having the energy or enough gumption to ride along with outlaws. Intimidating and starving his defenseless daughter for years, gambling, and staying drunk are more his style. He's a coward. He'll surface sooner or later. Don't ya worry! A hungry dog always returns to the food dish. He still owns the run-down little place where he and Mary Ann were living. He'll come back to it, and I'll be ready to pick him up when he does.

"For the life of me, I can't figure how he came to own that piece of land, but the bank swears it's free and clear and the taxes are paid. Why hasn't he gambled it away already? It doesn't make much sense considering BB's propensities. I keep thinking there has got to be some reason he's held on to it, but I haven't come across one yet."

"I've been wanting nothing more than rounding up these particular outlaws, but my priorities have changed today. I do want to ride out with you, but it conflicts with big trouble brewing here on the ranch. This is not the right time for me to leave. I'm needed here 'til things get handled. Then, I can focus on Mary's attackers. Yet, I'm sorely tempted to ride out with you if the perfect chance to catch the bastards is now. I'm being ripped apart in two different directions. I have faith in Smith and Coley to handle things here. They are more than capable of holding down the fort for a few days without me. Reluctantly, I'll leave with you tonight."

"Figured you'd be chomping at the bit to get your hands on 'em! Collect your gear and grub. We should leave within the hour."

Grey was always prepared to make a quick run. Never knowing when he'd be called to duty by the Rangers, his gear, ammunition, and camp grub were packed and ready. It was stored along with his tack and bedroll in the barn. All he had to do was grab a rash of bacon from the cellar, pilfer the biscuit tin, fill his canteens with fresh water, and gather his weapons. He'd throw on his hat, coat, and badge and be ready to ride.

With trepidation, he jotted a quick note to Mary Ann letting her know he had to leave suddenly but not why, and he made no mention of JD. He was concerned she'd be upset to know the reason he was leaving. Upstairs he rousted Coley out of bed and filled him in on what was up. He reinforced the need to guard and protect the family until he could get back.

Grey made a quick stop at Smith's house to let him know he'd be gone for a few days at the most. He and Smith agreed together the trip was important. Smith promised his brother the family's safety was the most pressing responsibility for him at home, and he and Coley would guard them with their lives. They could focus on reeling Wisteria in when he got back.

CHAPTER 21

———◆◦❖◦◆———

Greyson Byrd ◆

The Texas tallgrass parted like water as JD's and Grey's mounts pushed through the sea of grassland. The soft brushing whisper was familiar to the men and the seasoned horses. The rustling rhythm was conducted by the speed and even pace of the two horses. Being a few more hours before sunrise, collars were pulled up as barriers against the penetrating fall chill. They figured to catch up with the posse by dawn when it stopped to let the men eat and sleep for a few hours. All the horses would be ready for water, rest, and a chance to graze.

JD and Grey were ready to catch up with them and close their own eyes for some winks. One fire would be set to warm by, fry bacon, and make coffee to drink with cold biscuits. After this, until the outlaws were overtaken, the posse wouldn't risk the light of another fire being seen. It would be cold camps with jerky, dry biscuits, canned tomatoes, beans, peaches, and such. Each man toted his own supply of victuals and canteens of water.

JD and Grey rode along engrossed in their own private

thoughts. A dead serious purpose had settled over the two old friends several miles back. Seasoned men riding toward possible battle were predisposed to have focused reflections and guarded apprehensions. Riding into a myriad of unknown variables makes a man take inventory of what he could lose if things go sour.

Senses were sharpened to a higher level of cautiousness. Staying aware of surroundings would be the norm from here on out. Both men were set like hair triggers. Being careless and inattentive could get a man on prairie patrol killed. Every sound both near and far away, hovered on the peripheral of their awareness. Trained men could detect even the slightest, misplaced sounds. Keen senses on the prairie saved lives.

The two horses had ridden together on similar, covert missions. They were equally tuned into the natural environment, the unknown dangers ahead, and worked as a fine-tuned team. They were mindful and loyal to their riders' body languages, tensions, and directions. An exceptional horse was as important to a cowboy's survival as a fast and steady gun hand.

At times like this, Grey sought solace in the enormity of the star-studded Texas sky. This being a clear night, the expanse sparkled with multitudes of twinkling stars with no beginning or ending. The pure glory of it all brought to Grey's mind God's promise to Abraham in the Old Testament. The Lord promised to multiply his descendants until they outnumbered the stars. How high would the number grow?

A shooting star streaked across the vastness. He automatically made a wish. It was a habit taught to him by his ma long ago. How could one tiny orb sailing across the sky help with circumstances faced by one insignificant cowboy on the earth? Nevertheless, he never missed a chance to wish upon a star. He smiled thinking of Mary Ann who would no doubt have a storybook tale ready from the

Greek Myths. She'd have an entertaining tale of how shooting stars came to be and why they were associated with granting wishes. He'd have to remember to ask her.

She had a knowledge of the ancient myths. These fictitious accounts explained everything known to man. They were her happy places of escape, and she used them like bandages. Each one covered a hurt, an injustice, instances of fear and examples of separations. She understood perfectly they were imaginary and did not confuse them with God's truths. They were just diversions helping to deal with unpleasant realities. Now, she even had him thinking on fantasies of the fictitious gods ruling over a fictitious world in total chaos.

He had to admit they were entertaining with chariots racing across the sky, flying horses, and heroic superheroes like Thor wielding a heavy hammer as a weapon. What if all of mankind's woes could be locked in Pandora's box? It was inevitable a Medusa would always come along to free the troubles to wreak havoc on the innocents. Wisteria would make a believable Medusa. It was easy to imagine her with long squirming snakes for hair.

Mary had even renamed the white horse, Pegasus. Dang, if he hadn't started calling him Pegasus too! The name suited him. She likened Grey to the slayer of monsters who rode the white horse in the Greek Myths. He was pleased Mary Ann thought of him as her personal slayer of monsters. On his way to join the posse made him feel like the title.

She also talked a lot about the scriptures; the one true God and His angels. Grey believed in God and knew about the angels, but Mary Ann had a way of seeing them all around her. His girl even had him thinking about angels with a different perspective. She believed opportunities waited to be opened by faith. How could he argue with her? Perhaps God's angels helped Mary Ann to endure until it was the right time to send him, a lowly man, to rescue her.

Mary Ann had changed his way of seeing life, and he

liked the new perspective. How could a young girl influence a hardened man like himself in such profound ways? Until Mary, the blessings he'd been taking for granted hadn't seemed like much. Now, he was inspecting each one more closely and realizing the abundance he had and giving thanks to God. She made him a better man.

Beth's death and Mary Ann's resilience made him realize the value of time. He now treasured the moments instead of allowing them to pile up and be forgotten. Mary Ann had the enviable ability to find good in most things and learn lessons from the bad. This gift of attitude had allowed her to land on her feet and keep moving forward. How had he been stumbling through life so blindly until she came along and made him wiser?

For some unfathomable reason, Grey's skin started crawling. He had a feeling of dread and a relentless itch to turn around. He couldn't keep from thinking he needed to get back to his family. Every mile taking him farther from Byrd Ranch was causing a clenching in his gut. He sensed something he couldn't put his finger on, but he felt a nagging pull. It was silly, and if he told JD, his friend would think he'd gone crazy.

He'd ridden away from problems at home, but common sense told him Smith and Coley, along with the hands, could cope with whatever was happening at the ranch. Mary Ann and Sari were priceless pearls belonging to him, but he was still a Texas Ranger. A Texas Ranger who was being pulled in two different directions, so he had multiple, "what-ifs," making up the kindling building a fire within him.

He prayed this campaign JD and he were riding into could be resolved quickly, and he'd find the closure Mary Ann needed. He vowed he'd then make it back to the ranch as fast as humanly possible. He'd have a hard time ever being persuaded to leave his family alone again after this.

CHAPTER 22

Franklin McGill, The White Comanche ✦

Franklin McGill worked and worried a piece of prairie grass stem backward and forward between his teeth. The stick was worn ragged and soft like a brush on one end from his nagging and gnawing. Right now, his mind was simmering in thought as he considered his next move. The Texas Rangers and bounty hunters were on his tail and getting too close. He respected their doggedness, but not if he was the target. Nothing good could come of being in the crosshairs of the Texas Rangers. What he chose to do now would be crucial.

As an outlaw, Frank had committed many trespasses against innocent people and some not so innocent. Theft, destruction of property, bodily harm, and killings came easily to a man with no conscience. He owned his crimes and didn't mind claiming them, but he wouldn't let himself be caught to face the consequences. A unique path allowing him to dodge trouble and totally disappear was perpetually available to him through the tapestry of his piecemeal heritage. The mixed blood flowing through his veins made it possible for him to live and thrive in two distinctly different cultures. He knew his way around and was accepted in either world even though they were constantly at odds with each other

What galled him was being forced from one life and pushed across the line into the other before he was ready. This time he was backed into a corner and temporarily stripped of his own free will. There was no other option but to flee white society and cross over into living as an Indian. The white man's culture was his through the bloodline of his Irish father. The Comanche culture was his through the bloodline of his maternal grandmother.

The power to vacillate seamlessly between the two vastly different identities had its advantages as well as its drawbacks. One was a more difficult way of existence than the other. When he was a child, his full-blooded Comanche grandmother went back and forth visiting her native people. She'd sensed something special in him and always took her grandson along on these journeys. He learned to be a young Comanche brave as thoroughly as he learned to be a young, educated white boy. Franklin McGill, the Irish boy, and Nacona, the Comanche boy, became one in the same. They were human chameleons.

Playing outlaw had been an entertaining diversion until the day it wasn't. He'd played too close to the fire, literally, and participated in a serious mistake resulting in red hot heat almost immediately. By association, he'd inadvertently gone along with James to kidnap the pretty, young girl they'd spotted digging through trash piles in Spur. He became guilty for a crime not even interesting to him.

He'd voiced no objection to cheating BB Barton out of his daughter. When James and Arliss beat the man in the alley, he'd witnessed it and still said nothing. He'd also known what James had in mind for the girl and didn't care. Frank hadn't even planned to stick around to observe the violation, but he was on the porch when the girl was roughly dropped off. This was the first time he'd actually gotten a good look at her. The girl's beauty, a look of innocence, and the way she held herself impressed him. He saw gentleness, intelligence, and a strength of will. He could see immediately; she was a fine lass who deserved better.

Stepping forward, he assertively told James this one was his to take. It wouldn't save her the beating coming later, but he could at least rescue her from violent sex at the hands of an uncouth outlaw. James wasn't happy, but he couldn't deny him the right. Frank had never once taken his turn with a female captive before. He was due, of course, and there wasn't a whole lot of argument James could give about him claiming her. Grudgingly, he had stepped outside giving Frank privacy to perform the sexual act. Afterward, the other two refused to leave until they'd beaten her senseless. Then, Arliss set the house on fire with her inside.

Unfortunately, this specific crime caught the interest of one tenacious United States Marshal hellbent on restitution and one Texas Ranger with clout. Their influences garnered backing from the state capitol and personal support from the Rangers. Now, Frank couldn't risk his life by sticking around waiting for the axe to fall. It was imperative he switch personas as soon as possible. Men hunting Frank McGill would have a hard time recognizing and apprehending Nacona, a revered Seer in the Comanche nation.

Franklin saw himself in a vision. He was standing with one foot in a grave and the other slipping precariously on shifting sand. He was struggling to get both feet on higher and firmer ground. This crystal-clear image came to him as he was propped in the splintered doorway of the dilapidated hideout. Learning from experiences he knew when to hold his cards and when to fold them.

The handwriting was on the wall once he'd been cut from the herd and labeled, The White Comanche, on wanted posters. Suddenly, this unwelcome moniker made him vulnerable, and he was feeling pressed. The rather theatrical sketch on the poster and a sort-of-somewhat accurate description made him infamous and bigger than life. If he remained on this side of the line, he'd probably be killed. How he'd finally been linked to his Indian ancestry was a bit of a mystery. A member of his estranged family must have outed him. Needless-to-say, it was quite a game changer!

His worth in reward value had grown exponentially even before the printing ink dried on the first wanted poster. White men had a lust derived from ignorance and fear for sticking it to an Indian, any Indian. Crimes, not even his, had been credited to The White Comanche. The notoriety fattened the pot until a small fortune was being offered for him dead or alive.

His propensity for being a loner made it easier for him to slip away quietly without a trace. Becoming more publicly transparent diminished his freedom considerably. He'd need to be very diligent because even small children were now on the lookout for him. The switch from cowboy outlaw to an Indian brave was at hand.

Since the latest papers on his head read, Dead or Alive, then obviously dead it would be. Dead was less bother because only a bloody head, fit for identification, had to be turned into the nearest sheriff's office. Ghastly as harvesting a head could be for civilized people, they were a greedy lot and willing to go to any length for money. A head in a sack paid off the same as a walking body, and it wasn't lethal. A head didn't need to be guarded, fed, or listened to for days.

Franklin could pass for either bloodline due to the hue of his sun kissed skin. He had more Irish blood than Indian. His maternal grandmother, Topsannah, was a full-blooded Comanche from a band in Northwest Texas. She was bought by an Irish trader which wasn't uncommon at the time due to white ladies being scarce. The first son she bore him was named Franklin, after his father, and he was a half breed. He grew up and married an Irish woman, and he also named his first son, Franklin.

Franklin McGill the Third, by birth, was three quarters Irish American and only one quarter Indian. Biased people disregarded the mathematical law of fractions taught in school. Three fourths being larger than one fourth was not honored when evaluating the worth of an individual's blood. Society was intimidated and frightened by even a drop of Indian blood. If a person of mixed ethnicity, could pass for white, things were simpler.

Franklin McGill was insanely intelligent. He was wily like a fox, limber as an athlete, and quick. His Comanche granny, whom he loved dearly, made sure he knew the ways of his ancestors. His father, whom he respected, made sure he fit well with upper class society and got the best knowledge education offered. Thanks to both influences, he knew and understood their languages fluently.

The now infamous breed was standing in the doorway of the weathered shack, one hand above his head, bracing himself on the splintery door facia. The grass stem in motion was the only tell he was nervous. He wasn't fooled by the false peace of the serene view before him. All hell was about to break loose, and he could see and hear it. Being a Comanche Seer, his sensory receivers were amplified, and he could feel the changes blowing in the wind. He could smell death, feel its heaviness, and was certain it was only hours away. The velocity of pending chaos was gaining speed.

This rare and valuable gift of knowing things beforehand was inherited from his grandmother. She had foreseen on the day of his birth he was destined to live in two worlds. She prepared him in his people's ways. She taught him to understand his power of prophecies and how to use it. His visions had saved him many times. He'd be long gone before death could catch him.

The Shallow Water area on both sides of the North Fork River had been a safe cover to winter. The tiny cabin sat abandoned, isolated, and hidden. The condition told it had been given up to nature long ago. The brush was swallowing it and making it almost invisible, but it wouldn't keep the tenacious law dogs from finding it. Frank had become bored as hell here anyway. The two stupid idiots riding with him were no longer useful. He'd be on the trail well before sunrise. He didn't have to be a seer to know only one of the men would awaken to another morning. He was going to make quick work of killing Arliss before he rode out, leaving James behind.

He'd come full circle once again. It always came around to a similar finish, but always with a different twist. He was going back near the New Mexico border to find the brothers of his Comanche people. What was left of his granny's small band would be camped near Portales. They knew of his bravery and thirst for blood. He would be welcomed. He was curious about the baby child he'd sired with the Warrior Woman.

Bounty hunters and Prairie Patrolmen hesitated to ride directly into a party of Comanches for any reason. It would be like striking a hornet's nest. The Comanche killed just to be killing. Their ways of slaughtering gave them great pride. Causing prolonged pain was an art form to them. The women were the worst for dispensing torture. A few were so fierce; they were trained as warriors and rode into battle with the men.

He'd hidden among them before. He'd helped them hunt, protect their land, and annihilate entire Apache tribes. Many of the Comanche people were dead now too. It was not due to warring but to the deadly disease settlers had introduced to them. They had no defenses with which to fight off illnesses like the smallpox and cholera.

His plan to leave James alive was an offering to appease the law dogs and give them a story to tell. Killing Arliss would be a pleasure. He'd only tolerated him this long for the grunt work he could be bullied into doing. Arliss would be bled out before the sun even thought about coming up again. Let the buzzards and scavengers of the law collect the bounty on his stinking head. Let them chase James down like a rabid dog and hack his head off too.

Outlaw James ✦

James waking up to the permanent red grin sliced across Arliss's neck was a freak show. Then to realize his own knife had been used and was left driven into Arliss's heart had totally spooked him. It scared him shitless. Frank had been able to take his sticker right from under his nose without a sound. He feared Arliss's ghost was left behind as soon as he realized he'd been sleeping with the dead man. Frank could just have easily killed him too. The thought caused him to panic.

A quick look around told him Frank had not only butchered Arliss but also cleared out all the money and most of the provisions. The loses made him madder than hell. Dazed and confused, James ran around the shack in a frenzy grabbing anything of value. Sudden terror produced a burst of energy into James's system but did nothing to sharpen his ability to think. Rational thoughts flew out the window. In the aftermath of the initial shock, his whole body started shaking.

He had no idea Frank hated Arliss enough to kill the fool. They'd kept him around because he could be coerced into doing the heavy work. It was a plus he loved setting things on fire. Otherwise, the man was as dumb and useless as a dead bug, and the one eye made him a liability. He was too easily identified. James didn't care Frank had killed Arliss, but he'd assumed the two of them would stick together and split Arliss's share of the loot.

What a joke on James! He never saw this betrayal coming. His partner had run off and left him here with almost nothing. He ended up with a mount and tack, a little grub, and his gun, but only a few cartridges had been left behind.

He was leaving immediately, headed Southwest to Big Bend and the Mexican border. He'd winter in a border town and get lost. It would be hard getting there on the one poor horse, but maybe he'd find a replacement to steal.

CHAPTER 23

Mary Ann Byrd ✦

Mary, called away on business.
Didn't wake you. Tend to Sari.
I'll be back sometime, Grey

Mary Ann read and reread Grey's vaguely worded missive. He'd left it propped against the lamp in the center of the kitchen table. She'd discovered it the morning after he'd come to her room. His attention had made her feel special. He'd given her reason to believe he might truly love her someday. She'd dared to hope. The few, impersonal words he'd scrawled on the small slip of paper caused her to doubt it. She'd allowed his unexpected visit to let her dream.

Hopes and dreams were only imaginary. They were too illusive to be counted as real. The written words were a good reminder she shouldn't count on anyone. Forgetting this threatened her chances of personal survival. She'd put her heart at risk, and now it was cracked wide open. She stored the paper in her pocket during the day and tucked it under it her pillow at night. Mary had unfolded, refolded, and worried the thin scrap so many times the creases were beginning to tear apart just like her heart was ripping into more pieces each time she reread Grey's note. The penciled words were smudged by her index finger tracing each one over and over.

The short message held no details or room to be misinterpreted. She could clearly read between the lines. Her mind analyzed what was there. She filled in the rest by inserting her own words into Grey's mouth. Here were the facts as she saw them. He'd left her on her own and told her to take care of his precious baby girl. He'd abandoned Mary with his family and in his home. He had deserted her. The baby she carried would bear Grey's honorable name. She'd asked God for this, and He sent Grey. This should be enough. How could she not accept God's infinite wisdom and His gifts graciously?

Mary Ann realized she was being unfair. What could be wrong about having hope in the power of God? She'd always loved God, and His grace brought her here. If she was feeling sorry for herself, then it was her problem. She'd try harder to do her part, be thankful, and not expect more. Just because she'd mostly experienced men at their worst did not mean Grey was deceitful. Tearing down the thick, impenetrable wall of protection she'd raised around herself was what God wanted her to do. She must destroy the wall to give Grey a chance to enter. God would be dependable to do the rest.

A stoic resolve to tell Belle about the note came over Mary Ann. She'd been a worry to her sister-in-law the last three days by walking around depressed. Belle had tried her best to explain to her the hard, erratic lives of Texas Rangers. If she heard it one more time, Mary might scream.

"They're always being called away suddenly and most often in the middle of the night. Many is the time there isn't a moment for a ranger to spare on saying goodbyes or writing notes. It's a wonder they don't have a stash of prewritten letters so one can be pulled out and plopped on a table at the drop of a hat. It's always the same old story. Grey will ride in as soon as the mission is completed and not before.

"Mary, the rangers' women are the ones left behind to tend the home fires and be there when they return. Grey's an exceedingly kind and thoughtful man, so when he gets back, talk to him. Tell him how you felt when he left. Communicating will help you to figure this out together."

She'd quit giving Belle her full attention. She only listened with one ear now, because she'd heard too many variants of Belle's reassurances and efforts to soften the disappointment of his disappearance. Mary couldn't be honest and tell her she feared he'd run out on her for good. She was afraid he'd left because he'd gotten what he wanted, a new wife to take care of Sari. His goal had been reached. The scrawled note didn't make her think he'd be back anytime soon. She wasn't going to watch the road for him to return.

Understanding why Grey left didn't lessen Mary Ann's distress, but she could still treasure the way he'd treated her the night before. His gentleness had wrapped around her like a soft, warm blanket. For a little while she'd forgotten the sole purpose of her being here. He needed a wet nurse so badly he'd married one. She'd deceived herself into believing Grey wanted her.

At least Mary had a loyal friend in Sunny. He'd-appointed himself as her personal guard and companion and was her constant shadow. He followed her everywhere and even slept in her bedroom. The dog went with her to visit Pegasus in the main barn several times a day. It was a good place for Mary to go and be alone. The horse and dog soothed her and kept her company.

She'd been going there lately to replay the moment Grey entered her bedroom and closed the door behind him. He'd surprised her. At first, she'd been cautious, but he'd soon made her feel safe, wanted, and even desirable. His acceptance filled her with joy. The happiness lingered right up to the moment she'd found the note and realized he was gone.

The sweet caresses, kisses, and words turned out to be nothing but pleasing gestures. What she'd mistaken for genuineness was nothing more than a man being a man. He was indeed kinder than most, but she still got hurt. How could she have been so naive?

She crammed the note back into her pocket. The dark kitchen was closing in on her and breathing was getting harder and harder. She needed air. Her breaths were too short, too fast, and too shallow. The threat of suffocating panicked her, and she bolted without thinking from the front door. Sunny followed on her heels. Mary desperately needed to hide in the barn. Once outside, she gulped the crisp fall air until fear of collapsing turned into a dull ache in her chest.

The dark mouth of the barn drew her closer to promised privacy. Sunny ran ahead of her now. He knew exactly where she was headed. He and Pegasus were the only two, true companions she had in the world. Thankfully, she'd nursed Sari before coming downstairs and wouldn't be needed for a while. The baby was full and satisfied after eating and had fallen right back to sleep. Dawn was a while away yet, and no one was out stirring but her.

Feeling sorry for herself never served her well. It only distracted her and made her weak. She was well-acquainted to setbacks and could usually just skip over the self-pity part. Though this kink in the rope was bitter, she'd get past it. To be honest, she was the happiest she'd been in her whole life and would concentrate on blessings. Sari gave Mary great joy and purpose. Belle welcomed her here. Mary Ann liked helping with the house chores and the repetition of them. Her room was lovely beyond anything she could ever have imagined. She had pretty clothes, books, and feminine fancies.

She'd been given the supplies to make clothes, blankets, and nappies to prepare for her own baby. Belle was good-naturedly teaching her to sew and knit. One evening Grey had found her hemming a little blue blanket. He'd brought out Beth's personal sewing box for her to use. She cherished the latched box and its generous contents. It was a thoughtful thing for Grey to do.

The inside of the dank barn was much chillier than the brisk outside air. A coldness encompassed her body reaching clear through to her bones. A shiver played along her spine. The fall temperatures were turning colder, and a fine mist was coming down now. In her hurry to get out of the house, she'd hardly noticed the discomfort, but now chided herself for leaving the shawl and bonnet behind. She'd stormed out in a state of panic, and they'd been left inside. They wouldn't do much good still hanging on a peg by the door.

An ominous, foreboding cloud formed over her. She dismissed it as her imagination. However, it steadily grew in its weight. All of Mary's senses were alerted when Sunshine's ears perked, and he came to an abrupt stop, forcing her to go still. A menacing growl rumbled from down deep in his throat, and the hair on his back stood up. The pungent smells of animals, fresh hay and leather mingled together almost making her miss the most familiar smell. Whiskey! She smelled a pungent whiff of liquor! It was the unmistakable stench of whiskey! She'd been exposed to it all of her life, but she'd never smelled it here on the Byrd Ranch.

Not soon enough, all thoughts of visiting Pegasus fled, and they were replaced with prayers. She wanted out! She begged God for Him to get her out of the barn and back to the safety of the house. She'd walked freely into a trap. Just as she started to pivot and backtrack, thick, rough, sausage fingers gripped her ear pulling Mary Ann almost to the floor of the barn. The delicate skin ripped, and the dampness of blood trickled down her neck.

The other fat, meaty hand grabbed one arm and hauled her up causing pain in her shoulder. She was pulled by the ear until she had to stand on her toes. Before she could register exactly what was happening, she was face to face with pa breathing his nasty breath of decay into her face. The stench of his unwashed body and dirty clothes filled her nose. A dread akin to terror froze her brain rendering her unable to speak audible words. A ludicrously feeble squeal escaped her mouth instead. It opened it enough to allow room for a disgusting rag to be jammed inside.

During this, Sunny had commenced with a ferocious barking and jumping with all four feet soaring in the air. The ignorant ogre kicked out a foot making solid contact with the dog's head. Sunny yelped shrilly. Unrelenting, he came back again with his forelegs high in the air. The underbelly of his stretched body was met with a sharp-toed boot knocking him down and the air from his lungs. After a moment, Sunny started whimpering. There was blood where the boot had made contact. Sunny did not make another sound or move again.

In all the uproar, she'd been able to cough and dislodge the soiled rag out of her mouth.

"Sunny," Mary called out, but only Pegasus answered her.

"Pa, stop! Don't hurt him again, please stop."

It was too late. BB's foot was already on the path to boot him in the side as he lay silently on the barn floor.

The noise and commotion had barn animals restlessly pawing at their enclosures. Mary Ann recognized Pegasus's presence amid the pandemonium. Her legs gave way beneath her causing Pa's grip to loosen. She fell hard to the ground and crab crawled backwards, dragging her bottom. She tried her absolute best to get away but was stopped short when her head butted hard against Pegasus's stall.

"I've got ya now girlie girl! Did ya think I wouldn't come

for ya? Ain't ya somethin' to lay eyes on in that there purty dress? You're all high-falutin' like a dressed-up pig. Ain't ya?"

Pa laughed sarcastically. He reached down and ripped the bodice to her waist and the pearl buttons flew making little noises of contact if they hit something. I'm gonna make you pay for disappearing on me. You can count on it! First, I gotta get us far away from here. That there big, white horse knows ya, Mary. It's the one you ride. Ain't it? I seen ya."

At that very moment, Pegasus reached out over the gate and snuffled the top of her head bringing Mary Ann some clarity. By then, Pa was already tying her hands behind her back and her ankles together. The chance to get away was gone.

"You don't belong here, Pa! Haven't you caused enough pain to me? I'm done with you! I thought it was over! Please, ride on out. They're looking for you. I won't tell anybody you were here. I promise. I'll even see if I can scrape up some money and food to give you before you go. Get out of here while you still can. The law won't quit hunting until they find you."

"Maybe they are lookin', but maybe I'm smarter than them. Ya' belong ta me, Mary. Ya always have. Ya'll always belong ta me! Don't fergit it no more! I own ya.

"The realer question I'm wonderin' on is how'd ya come to be here on this fancy ass ranch?"

"I live here Pa. This is my home now. I'm married to Ranger Grey Byrd. He'll kill you if he finds you anywhere near me!"

"Cain't hurt me. He's gone, not even here. He rode out in the dark with'n the nosey marshal from Spur a while back. They was in a hurry, not likely ta be back fer a spell by the looks of their packs. Yer dear ol'pappy's been a watchin' this place lookin' fer a chance when no one was around ta grab you'in. I'm gonna' give ya a what fer later. Yer a slow learner, girlee. Yes, siree! I need ta teach ya. Ya' cain't run 'n hide from yer pappy. I own ya!

"Say, heard talk you'se in tha fam'ly way a carry'n a bastard brat. Bet'n ya don't know who the father is, neither! A'ways figurin' ya fer a slut, jus' like yer no count ma."

"Don't talk about my mother! It's your fault I got this way, and you know it! You handed me over to those filthy men. You bet me in a game of cards! You lost me in a poker game, and you knew exactly what they were going to do with me.

"You're no longer my pa! You never were a pa to me. Leave here! Leave me be while you can! I'm not alone anymore. I've got people, a family. I'm happy for the first time in my life. I've got food to eat. I'm not hungry anymore. Grey will protect me from the likes of you."

"That so? I don't see 'nabidy nowhere around. Who's gonna stop me from takin' ya?"

Mary struggled against the tight ropes to no avail.

This had to be a nightmare she was stuck in. She tried to wake up but soon realized it was really happening. Why did she leave the safety of the house? She couldn't even remember anymore. Hadn't Grey warned her to stay close to the house? There was no chance to think or speak another word. A hard fist connected with her temple, blackening the light.

CHAPTER 24

Belle Byrd ✦

Belle was late getting to the main house this morning. She entered through the back door of the kitchen letting the screen door plop-bang behind her. The horizon was already marked with streams of pink, orange and yellow light announcing the sun would make its grand appearance soon. Smith told her Grey rode out in the middle of the night with JD on a chase. She thought this an inconvenient time for him to leave the ranch with the possibility of Wisteria lurking around, but she didn't say so. Who knew what the woman could pull next?

The house was dark, stone quiet, too still, and it made Belle hurt to be reminded Beth was gone forever. No more would she and Beth be cooking and laughing together again. Mary Ann was friendly company, but most often she went back to bed after Sari's first feeding to rest. She usually didn't come downstairs until after the baby fussed to be fed again.

Belle rattled pots, pans, and dishes getting the breakfast started by herself. Her husband and Coley would soon come in from the morning chores as hungry as bears. It was good to have familiar routines to keep her busy. She wanted Beth here though. Wishing wouldn't make it so.

The food had to be cooked and laid out in short order, so daydreaming would have to wait. The first things she'd done were stoke the fire in the cookstove and set a fresh pot of coffee to brew. This had to be done every morning before other tasks. By the time fluffy biscuits were baking in the hot oven, bacon was sizzling and popping on a top burner, and a thick, white pepper gravy was bubbling on another. She'd scramble a dozen hen eggs at the last minute in the flavorful bacon grease just the way the boys loved them.

Smith and Coley ✦

Right on time, just like clockwork, the two brothers were washing up on the back porch. The aroma of coffee and breakfast were calling them to the table. Belle smiled hearing their voices filtering into the kitchen from the porch. She couldn't make out the words exactly but enough to know they were talking about what Smith had to do insuring Wisteria couldn't set foot on the ranch without being seen. He reorganized a few of the ranch hands' schedules so one of them was always guarding the house. He'd warned everyone to stay armed and alert to anything out of the ordinary until told to stand down.

Coley would work on finding incriminating evidence today. He'd start with tearing Wisteria's upstairs bedroom apart looking for any clue left behind. He had other places to check on his list, but the upstairs room would be first. He'd talk to Doc next and then start looking in town where it would be a bit trickier not to be seen and draw attention.

"Wonder when Grey and JD caught up with the posse? Maybe they'll get lucky, and all this can be wrapped up soon."

"Well, Coley, luck can never be tallied until the end. If a

man's countin' on luck for a break, it'll never be there when he needs it. We've got our own fish to fry here."

"Yeah, suppose you're right. It might be the outlaws will have the luck this time around," Coley agreed.

"I'm planning on being a detective today. I like snooping around to catch bad guys, or in this case, a bad woman. There is no telling what things might turn up in the strangest places. It is interesting to try and get into the mind of a criminal--- think like he, or she, might think. I like to guess what the next move might be."

"Coley, maybe you're destined to be a Pinkerton agent. You don't have to go to Chicago to work. You could just be a reserve detective, working when needed, right here, where you understand the territory. Grey was considering this very thing a few years back. If you like digging around into crimes and getting paid for it, give it a thought, if the idea suits you."

"I might just look into it. Back to Wisteria, she's our immediate problem, Smith. There are three or four questions for us to consider. Is she capable of hurting our family right now? Did she murder Beth and her babies? For years, she's had the freedom of being considered one of the Byrd family. She knows a lot of details about us, our routines, and our habits. The third question is, has she been pulling the wool over our eyes all this time?

"It's hard to imagine anyone could do harm to their own cousin, especially, anyone as nice as Beth. I've never liked Wisteria, myself. I've always seen her as being sneaky. I never trusted her, but murder is question number four. Could she kill somebody?"

"I can't wrap my head around it either, Coley. Beth had a good heart. She nurtured all of us, like our own mother. If there's somethin' to find, I swear we're gonna' find it! If Wisteria murdered Beth, then I want a jury to have all the evidence it needs to hang her!"

Belle ◆

Monday was washday even with the weather looking and feeling like a blue norther was on the way. Rain had fallen earlier but had turned back into a fine mist. It all meant wearing a bulky coat, and the work would be harder. The wet clothes couldn't be hung out to dry today. They would be draped around the house to dry.

Belle was hoping Mary Ann would be down by the time the water was hot enough to start. It wasn't like her to lay-abed so long. She was still weak, pregnant, nursing, and sulking because Grey left. Still, she could be a lot of help, but if she was sleeping, her body needed the rest. Belle hadn't heard moving around upstairs, except for Coley. He wasn't kidding when he said he'd take Wisteria's room apart.

Ranch hands stacked wood and laid a fire waiting to be lit under the cast iron wash pot on Saturday. They filled it and the rinse pot with water too. Belle lit it before breakfast was cleared away. She also put beans on to boil and a roast in the oven for supper. On wash days, the brothers ate the noon dinner in the bunkhouse because washing took a big part of the day. Thank goodness Cookie did the washing for the cowboys,

Belle was getting uneasy Mary Ann might be sick. The strain of Wisteria's outburst yesterday had caused a lot of strain on everyone. The tension couldn't have been good for Mary. She'd go check on her if she didn't come down soon.

Sometime later, she heard the baby crying when she came in the house to lay out some damp clothes. Belle had been working outside, so she couldn't be sure how long Sari had been wet and hungry. When she didn't stop, and her cries became more pitiful, Belle ran to see about them both. She found Coley in the nursery clumsily changing a nappy with an uncomfortable look on his face.

"Why are you taking care of Sari? Where's Mary Ann?"

"I knocked on her door, but she didn't answer. I think this baby's hungry, Belle." Coley sounded frustrated by the whole situation. Babies obviously did not fall under his list of responsibilities.

Belle didn't bother with knocking first. She opened the door to Mary's room and barged right inside. The bed was made, but Mary Ann wasn't there. Something wasn't right.

"Coley, come here quick!"

He rushed out of the nursery carrying a fussy Sari who was trying desperately to find the right spot on his shirt to nurse. Coley awkwardly handed off the hungry baby to Belle like a hot potato.

"Where is she? What's going on? Start looking in every room."

Upstairs, doors started opening and closing. Every room was searched, even Coley's own bedroom. They were both calling their sister's-in-law name out. The uproar had Sari wailing louder. There was no sign of Mary Ann upstairs or downstairs.

"You go outside to find her, Coley. I'll see if Sari will take a little bit of warm cow's milk. I don't like this, Coley. Something is very wrong. Mary Ann makes a point to be the one tending Sari. Feeding her is not something she would miss."

Smith Byrd ✦

The hair on the back of Smith's neck stood up with the sharp ringing. The back porch triangle called anyone in hearing distance to the house in case of an emergency. He mounted his horse while he already had his gelding on the run. The house alarm was never sounded unless there was an injury, a fire, or catastrophic news. Speed and fear were foremost in his mind.

Smith had left a man sticking close to the house after breakfast. How could something bad have happened? He couldn't remember when his little brother had called him in before. Coley met Smith in the yard and from the look on his face, he knew this must be really bad news. He looked around for Belle but didn't see her anywhere, and fear for his precious wife overtook him

Smith started yelling before he dismounted. "Where's Belle?"

"She's gone, just gone, Smith!"

Smith almost vomited to think something had happened to his wife. "What do you mean gone? What's happened to Belle?"

"No! Mary Ann is the one gone, vanished! The man you posted by the house didn't see or hear anything. He only left for a while to do his perimeter check. He says things have been quiet.

"Belle and I searched the whole house upstairs, downstairs, the attic, the cellar, and all the other buildings. Pegasus is missing from the barn too, but Sunshine was lying in there hurt and bleeding. Cookie is working on him right now. There's been a struggle in the barn. There are a few things out of place, buttons scattered, and some blood. The wet morning has ruined most of the tracks.

"Mary Ann isn't down by the creek or anywhere on the grounds, I can see. Her shawl and bonnet are still hanging in the hall, but I found one of her slippers between the barn and side gate! I did find a few tracks, but between the damage the rain shower caused and the dense ground cover, they're hard to read. There are two sets of tracks leading out. I recognize a couple of Pegasus' hoof prints, but the other horse is not one of ours. Pegasus is definitely carrying the lighter load, so Mary must be riding him." Coley was breathless by the time all these words rushed out of his mouth.

Belle came out of the house, cradling the baby. Both their faces were red and puffy from crying but for different reasons. She leaned her weight against Smith's big frame, and her knees nearly buckled from the relief of seeing him. A circle of curious cowboys had formed. They were gathered around to find out what was wrong. Early arrivers were filling in the late comers with bits and pieces of the story they'd gathered. All were trying to talk at once, and chaos was the result.

They'd already been put on alert and cautioned about Beth's cousin, Wisteria Winters. Smith told them she was not to set foot on the ranch and to keep their eyes open for anything out of the ordinary. Now, they were speculating about this and sharing theories like a bunch of old hens. They were well-meaning, but nothing could make any sense midst the loud ruckus. Some had figured out Grey's wife was missing and needed to be found as quickly as possible.

Smith got everyone's attention by firing once into the air. Finally, it was quiet enough for them to hear him. The sudden blast caused Sari to commence crying again, and Belle turned to hurry away with her into the house. Smith stopped her from leaving.

"We're wasting time! Belle, I need you to tell me what's happened. Be as straight and clear with the details as you can. Don't leave anything out even if it's something you only think."

Sniffling, she forced herself under control and started recounting what she could recall.

"Mary Ann was late coming down this morning, and I figured she needed the rest. I thought getting so upset yesterday had taken a toll on her, so I never thought I needed to check on Mary. Then, the baby was crying just a while ago and wouldn't stop. I went upstairs to see if I could help. Something just didn't seem right. Mary's such a good mother. I found Coley in the nursery trying to take care of Sari by himself.

"We both had figured out by then something was amiss. I went into Mary's room. Her bed was made, but she was gone, just gone! Coley and I searched the upstairs, downstairs, and in the yard without finding her.

"Sari was fussing so hard for something to eat. I took her into the kitchen to try cow's milk. Coley kept looking for Mary Ann. I could hear him calling her name. Later, I heard the alarm sound and knew Coley was ringing it. knew then, for sure, there really was trouble!"

"Thanks, Belle. You can take Sari into the house now and calm her down.

"Don't anyone else walk around the house or go into the barn again until I have a chance to look. Fresh eyes can sometimes find something missed. When I clear it, some of you start on the outskirts of the yard and keep walking in larger and larger circles. Keep it up until you get far away from the house. Be looking for anything, any signs giving us a clue. There's got to be something.

"One of you go to the bunkhouse and see how Sunny is doing. Tell Cookie when he's done with the dog to make lots of coffee, sandwiches, and whatever, in case this takes a while. The bunkhouse will become our headquarters. Anyone needing food, drink or instructions report there. I'm gonna' send out two small search parties, and I'll ride with one of them. Coley, you stay here and stay on point. Anyone finds anything, fire your gun once into the air. If any of you locate Mary Ann, fire three times in the air and keep it up until you're answered back with shots!"

"This light rain and the cold wind whipping up won't work in our favor. Mary Ann's out there in this cold wind and mist with a norther getting ready to bear down on us. We know for sure she doesn't have anything warm to wear. She's got to be found. Hopefully, she'll be back here soon, but we may all be in for a long, hard day until we find her.

"Coley, send someone into town to tell the sheriff what's happened. Ask if he can round up some help."

CHAPTER 25

BB Barton ✦

BB Barton sat in the cold mist looking down on the ranch house and barns from behind rocks and brush above. This was a secluded vantage point allowing him to spy on the main grounds of the Byrd Ranch. Since Monday, he'd studied the comings and goings. Wisteria Winters sent him here to abduct Mary Ann. Now he'd seen how rich the Byrds were, and he was anxious to rip all this luxury away. It wasn't fair for the bastard child of a whore to fall into such a cozy deal. Damn her and her mother to hell! The thought of the woman's whelp falling into wealth filled him with anger.

The plot to steal Mary had all been set in motion when BB was rousted from his sleep in the hay loft on Sunday night. Wisteria came home from visiting her relatives, and she was madder than hades. She was pale like she'd just seen a ghost. The prissy woman wasn't her usual self. She'd generously brought good whiskey with her and began pushing it on him to drink. Once he got a buzzy head, she started firing questions at him. The drink loosened his lips freeing answers from his mouth best kept to himself.

He'd come four months ago to hide out in her little barn in Cap Rock. He thought he had the upper hand with all he knew about her crimes. He knew about the murders she'd committed, or at least the ones he'd helped her commit or cleaned up for her. He had enough to blackmail her to do what he wanted, but how quickly she'd applied leverage and turned the tables on him! This was one clever bitch. She took the upper hand from him in the blink of an eye.

The shrewd woman outfoxed him as easily as melting grease on a hot skillet. She made it crystal clear if he didn't keep quiet and march to her tune, she'd pin the murders solely on his head. She'd leave him holding the bag with no defense. Even in his drunk, foggy mind, with his low standards, and his lack of moralities he'd been shocked by the deceit and lengths this she-devil had gone to insure his allegiance. He never suspected she owned him hook, line, and sinker. She'd accumulated and manufactured enough evidence to keep him under her control.

BB was being manipulated like a puppet in a side show. No doubt, she was rich and bitch enough to cause him the grief she promised and more. He finally realized the power she held over him, and BB couldn't fight against it. Complying and following her orders was his only choice.

Once he sobered, he was stunned to realize she knew Mary Ann and expected him to kill her. She didn't want her to die outright either but to suffer and go out in a slow, painful death. She described in detail how she wanted it done. He wasn't sure why she had a bull's eye drawn on Mary's back. What he did understand was he'd have to do whatever Wisteria Winters said. She had him good and cornered.

Being blackmailed created quite the conundrum for BB. He had to keep the girl alive for his own evil reasons. Those bank records in Spur had to stay sealed. If he killed Mary, there was always a chance the sheriff with the big nose would find out she was dead. On her death, the homestead at Spur would be forfeited back to the original owner or his descendants per the sealed documents held in the vault.

BB had no intention of letting the place slip through his fingers so easily after all this time. It was the only thing he held of worth except his horse. This was quite a conundrum. He couldn't afford not to kill Mary, but neither could he afford to kill her. There had to be a way to work around this problem. He was going to figure out how to protect his own interests while satisfying Wisteria's demands. He needed some way to make Wisteria believe she was dead while she was still alive.

BB was supposed to murder her and dump the body in the old well hidden by an ocean of prairie grass. He didn't know how deep it had been dug, but Wisteria had a good start on filling it up. It was her go to place to dispose of kills whether they be man or beast. He'd followed her orders without question and done her bidding for years, because the money couldn't be beat. Most of the time, he never even had to work up a sweat. Except for keeping the mouth of the well tightly sealed shut so circling buzzards wouldn't call attention to the decaying bodies, there wasn't much work he had to do.

This would be one time she wasn't getting her way. He had no intention of killing Mary Ann. It was his secret she had to stay alive, but if he could arrange for her to disappear, Wisteria would be none the wiser. There was even a good chance this job was going to result in being paid twice. Wisteria had already told him the town where she'd mail his money. There would be an additional hefty bonus for killing Mary. She said she never wanted to see him again afterward. All he had to do was pick up an envelope addressed to him after the job was finished and ride out of the territory. The way he saw it, he was going to get paid well regardless.

When he sobered, he made plans of his own to rendezvous with Comancheros who bought females of childbearing age to sell or trade to Comanches in New

Mexico. They needed them to breed babies and build up their numbers. Many of their people had died from diseases in the past few years brought in by settlers. Comancheros might even pay up for a girl like Mary who was already bred. The Comanche weren't picky about whose kids they raised. Some would be indoctrinated into their culture, and some would be used as slaves.

The weather was changing abruptly from summer heat to erratic instabilities foretelling of fall. Today the sky to the north was a dark, purple-blue, and the wind from the north had picked up considerably blowing in a blue norther. By the feel of things, it would hit full force by the afternoon. He planned to grab the girl and be riding ahead of it before then. He wrapped his heavy coat and blanket around himself more tightly.

Empty bean cans laid where he'd tossed them along with three dead soldiers. One of those still had swallows of dark amber rot gut left in it, but the other two were drained dry. Various pieces of paper had blown into the brush and gotten trapped. BB's discarded litter field was typical of the way he lived his life.

BB watched and kept track of the comings and goings around the house and barns. He drank to pass the time and stay warm. A fire was too risky, so he stayed in a cold camp. He was anxious to grab Mary as soon as possible. She had predictable habits. Every afternoon, she sat on the front porch for a while. Once the little chit came out with a baby wrapped up in her arms. Wisteria had told him Mary was with child, but this baby must belong to the other lady he'd seen.

Mary gathered the eggs each day about the same time. She made predictable trips to the big barn at least twice a day without fail. Often, she'd lead a big white horse out and brush him in the sun, talking to him and petting him affectionately.

Getting his hands on her when she went to the barn was

his best bet. He'd slip into the building and grab her inside since the hands were busy elsewhere during the day. He would take her fast and get away before anyone knew she was gone. With any luck, it might be a while before she was missed.

A miserable, fine mist set in after midnight, and it turned colder. He was surprised to recognize the nosey marshal from Spur riding in and going to the door of the house. A peppering rain commenced just before he came out with another cowboy. They rode out in a hurry as soon as the second horse was saddled and led out of the barn. The two rode out headed north. The dampness had managed to work its way down his collar and into his shoes penetrating his cotton socks. He was getting too old for shit like this.

Before daybreak, BB did indeed have some luck. The shower stopped. Then his hackles rose as he watched the girl and dog rush out of the house and run to the barn. Never had he observed her leaving the house before daylight before. How fortuitous the lawman left a few hours earlier, and the lights were out in the house and bunkhouse. This was the break he'd been waiting so long to happen. The girl was alone under the cover of darkness with only him around to see her.

CHAPTER 26

---◆-◌✛◌-◆---

Greyson Byrd ◆

Grey's eyes were locked on the lone rider in the distance. When he caught up with the son-of-a-bitch, the count would be two down and one to go. He didn't intend to stop with the three outlaws though, BB Barton had to pay the price for what he'd done to his daughter. Finding the one-eyed thief and murderer dead in the shack only a couple of hours before was disappointing and anticlimactical. He had some questions he wanted to ask. His cold, dead body robbed Grey of the primal satisfaction of watching him die.

Seeing the man with his throat laid open from one ear to the other was shocking, but Grey had seen similar scenes before. The victim had bled out making the pallor of the dead man's skin eerily gray and waxy. It contrasted with the darker expression of awareness frozen on his thin lips. It was one of abrupt surprise as if he'd just recognized his killer. His one eye was wide open as if he was still seeing his attacker's face. An arm was propped up at the elbow with his hand bent at the wrist pointing an index finger in the direction of Grey, but more likely at nothing. If only the dead could talk!

At this moment Grey was in hot, relentless pursuit of the man he was chasing. It would go easier, or at least quicker, if the man would just stop in his tracks and face the inevitable. The ranger was pushing his appaloosa, Spanish Flight, so hard that he had out distanced himself from the rest of the riders. They were eating his dust, but Grey sensed JD's big black gaining on Spanish Flight. He knew his friend was trying to reach the outlaw first. He was determined to save Grey from killing him outright. Grey considered this outlaw was his alone to strike down. The privilege of vengeance for his wife was his right.

Before Grey killed him, he intended to get some answers to questions eating away at him. Then, he wanted him to know whose woman he'd violated. Grey needed him to know exactly who was putting the bullet in his head. This worthless piece of shit was going to see hell today! Never again would he have the chance to sully another innocent girl.

When Grey was in range, the desperate man turned in the saddle aiming his gun as best he could. His shot went wild shooting a hole in nothing but the choppy wind. The second bullet hit home and grazed painfully across Grey's flesh. Hardly registering the shock of the impact or deterring the ranger's determination, he spurred his lather covered stallion forward urging him to give more. True to his nature, Spanish Flight answered the demand for speed with all he had. Grey felt him kicking into a higher gear flying over the prairie grass taking his master wherever he asked.

As if happening in slow motion, Grey watched as the horse ahead stepped in a hole causing him to dip low toward the leg's shoulder. The gun flew high out of the criminal's hand. He screamed in pain as the poor horse met hard with the ground, crushing the rapist and murderer under its full weight.

Spanish Flight intuitively sensed the end of the chase. Digging in his hind feet, obscured by a thick cloud of Texas dust, his butt almost dragged the ground. He skidded to an impressive stop with no wasted yardage. By this time, Grey had already evacuated his seat landing in his own haze of dust. He was already face to face with his target. He had his shooter aimed at the trash. Within moments, JD had a calming hand on his friend's shoulder feeling the powerful trembling rippling through Grey.

"Don't, Ranger! You're better than this. Don't make a big mistake here!"

"Damn ya to hell, ya sorry, lowlife bastard. Ya piece of horse shit! Why? Why'd ya hurt her? She was just a girl. She is my wife!"

JD quickly evaluated the condition of the fallen horse. The lathered gelding had a badly busted leg with the bone sticking through his skin. His wind was spent and blown. He was struggling to breathe. The poor animal was in misery. The marshal mercifully dispensed a quick, well-placed bullet ending the animal's suffering. Grey was so caught up in the heat of his own emotions, he didn't even flinch at the sharp report of the bullet hitting near his head. Even when the broken man trapped under his horse issued a squall of pain, it didn't register with Grey.

"Don't ya' dare pass out on me now, you son-of-a-bitch! You're not the Indian. I take it you're the one called James. How many times did ya rape my wife? How many times did ya hit her?"

Blinking, the pain-crazed man asked with a raspy voice, "Who's yer wife? Who're ya? I've poked a bunch 'a wifs...pft..."

"You're gonna feel how hot the fire is in hell any minute! My name's Ranger Grey Byrd! BB Barton's girl is my wife. She was an innocent young lady when ya got hold of her!"

"Ne'er...liked secon's...the Comanch...nailed firs'. I jus' played on 'er sum'."

"What about the one-eyed man ridin' with ya?"

"Arliss jus' beat 'er. Set a fire…his dead. Fra'k got 'im good.

Grey's knee was now soaked in the blood oozing out from beneath the dying man. He wasn't sure if it was from the horse, James, or both. The outlaw was growing weaker and paler.

"Open your eyes! Damn ya! Look at me! Don't ya' die. She's my woman, my woman. I'm the one who's gonna kill ya!"

Without seeing, James whispered in barely audible puffs of air. "Ta late, rang'r. I'm…al'redi…go…n…," and so he was; gone no doubt to the pit of hell and gagging right now on Satan's sulfur.

Grey threw his head up letting out a loud tired, exasperated howl. He'd wanted to put an end to him by his own hand. Only then did he realize JD was kneeling by him with his arms fast around his shoulders. JD wouldn't have allowed him to commit murder, but his best friend understood why he wanted to end him. What a friend! It was best the man died without Grey's help. Later the ranger would thank JD for stopping him. The rest of the men rode up in silence taking in the gruesome scene. Two of the bounty hunters had already started the grisly task of harvesting the head. Another held the sack. Arliss's head had already been bagged.

CHAPTER 27

———◆-◦❖◦-◆———

T he marshal and the ranger split with the posse after the excitement was over and headed toward home. They rode only a short distance before stopping to tend Newman and Spanish Flight. They needed to be brushed, tended, fed, watered, and rested overnight. Greyson's appaloosa had burned his heels sliding up short by the outlaw and his fallen horse. Grey greased the abrasions with bacon grease for it was all he had. He wrapped them in bandages and would do better by him at Byrd Ranch. The injury could have been far worse considering how hard he'd pushed his horse. Spanish Flight was a performance mount. He always gave Grey every bit he asked and more.

Grey was favoring one arm because of the flesh wound. JD had cleaned, doctored, and bandaged it soon after it happened. It could have been worse, so Grey was lucky. There was no need for a cold camp tonight, and the two friends feasted on fried bacon, hot biscuits, gravy, and peaches. They'd had quite enough cold canned beans for a while. After stuffing themselves, JD pulled a couple of cheroots out of his saddle bags and the pint of whiskey he carried for medicinal purposes. The horses weren't the only ones who'd earned a little relaxation and rest after the afternoon's intense adrenaline rushes.

The cowboys savored the smokes and passed the bottle back and forth looking up at the vast sky in silence. A blue norther had blown through a few days ago. Its cold air had been left behind. They would stoke the fire all night and sleep close to it for warmth.

JD broke the silence. "Ya already love her. Don't ya ole son?"

"It's hard not to admire Mary Ann. When she answered the door on the first day, I could see she was special. You'd already set me up, JD, by sharing her soulful story. It didn't hurt none she was the only woman who could save Sari.

"I recognized her innocent beauty from the inside out. She was so beautiful, and God help me, I wanted her. I fought the feeling because of Beth. Beth was a great woman, and I loved her. I still do. God knows I still do! Feeling love for Beth is the only way I can live with myself, but Mary Ann needs me, JD. If any woman ever needed love and protection, it's her. Don't misunderstand me, I can see how strong and self-sufficient she is and give her credit for it. There's something else about her though. She makes me want to be with her, take care of her. I missed my chance to save Beth, but I can prevent Mary Ann and the baby growing inside of her from being harmed by anyone.

"She fills my heart. It's hard to explain. I can't find the right words, but I swear I'm going to pour myself into this marriage. If I don't already love her, I will."

"Maybe hard for you to explain, but I think I get it. Even I came to admire her strength and how hard she worked to recover from the injuries. Once I pieced together her whole heartbreaking past, I was ashamed for not ever noticing her predicament. I could have helped.

"When you came in the night looking for Mary Ann, I had

mixed feelings. On one hand I was afraid she'd get hurt, on the other hand, I knew you and the ranch were the best possible fit.

"When I found you still up the other night and listened to you talk, I heard the words of a besotted man. Innocence, sweetness, gentleness, beauty, and strength are a beguiling combination in a woman.

"When the doctor told her she was pregnant, her concern was only for the baby, not herself. She didn't cry or wring her hands but instead met the challenge head on. It was what it was, and she stepped up. The more life goes against her, the more backbone she reveals."

JD was looking at the clouds passing by overhead. He was lost in thought for a minute.

"I'm praying God and my Aunt Polly are sending me a girl with the determination Mary has. This country is hard on its women. They fare better if the mettle is there to get right back up when something knocks them down."

"Do ya know what day it is?" Grey asked.

"Let's see, I think it's Friday, no, must be Saturday, nope, Friday, I think."

"It's been too long. I've been away from the ranch too long. I should've stayed put. Wisteria busting into the house like a cyclone on Sunday has haunted me. Five or six days is enough time for most anything to have happened. It was poor judgment to ride off and leave my family in danger."

Grey Byrd had a restlessness churning in his gut. He couldn't shake the confounded feeling something wasn't right. While tracking the outlaws, he'd been able to push his concerns to the back of his mind. Putting Arliss and James down was a temporary high. Once the adrenaline wore off, a cold fear replaced it. He'd always trusted his instincts, but he hoped he was wrong this time.

Mary Ann, Sari, and his family flooded Grey's thoughts. They were his responsibility. Trying to ease his worries, he'd shared his concerns with JD. It helped to finally be headed back in the direction of home, but they weren't traveling fast enough to satisfy Grey. Every mile covered compounded his feeling something was wrong. He didn't know what he was going to find waiting for him.

Mary and Sari were who mattered to him the most. He'd made up his mind to turn in his badge and stay close to home after this. He'd made his last mission for the Texas Rangers. Grey had decided this when the bulk of the posse kept on trailing the third outlaw. He'd felt no duty or pull to go with them.

It was unlikely The White Comanche would allow himself to get caught. The breed was cunning and had learned the Comanche tricks of survival. He'd cover his trail and deliberately leave signs to follow going nowhere. The mismarked trail would cost the posse time and cause frustration. The harder they chased, the harder he'd be to find. Catching a man like him would take a different approach.

Dog tired and dragging their tails behind their legs, Grey and JD rode into the yard of Byrd Ranch near dusk. Everything looked deserted, and the stillness caused Grey's hair to stand up on the back of his neck. The silence was surreal. Where was the activity around the bunkhouse? This being a Friday night, the two men should be hearing guitars, harmonicas, horseshoes being thrown, and laughter. Grey's instinct had been right after all. Something was very wrong.

The two friends' eyes met. Things weren't right here. Grey dismounted and handed the reins over to JD without a word passing between them. He left JD to tie the horses to the hitching rail. He cleared the porch steps in two strides of his long legs. He held his hand on his sidearm just in case.

CHAPTER 28

━━━━━◆━❧✠❧━◆━━━━━

"**W**here is everybody?" Grey called out loudly. As soon as he'd pulled the door open, the intoxicating aroma of freshly baked bread hit him. Next, the sound of a chair scraping on the wooden floor, then hurried footsteps coming from the direction of the kitchen set him walking that way. Belle ran at him like a squirrel climbing a tree and launched into his arms. He barely caught her. She was crying uncontrollably, and he couldn't make, heads nor tails, of the garbled words and incomplete sentences coming out of her mouth.

Grey was fearing whatever had Belle out of her mind. His heart was pumping so hard, he felt it hitting the wall of his chest with each beat. He hugged his hysterical sister-in-law close to calm her. His grip relaxed gradually as she began to settle. Putting her back on her feet, he placed both hands on her shoulders and gently shook her trying to help her focus.

"Belle! Belle, pull yourself together. You're okay now. Settle down, so I can understand what you need to tell me! Where is everyone? Where are Smith and Coley? Where are Mary Ann and Sari?"

Gulping air and hiccupping, she answered. "Smith's in and out coordinating everything, but, but he's been riding out by himself to search too. I don't expect him back until tomorrow, if even then. He's been doing his best, Grey. Coley's out making the rounds again. He should be back soon. He patrols every couple of hours. So far things have been quiet."

"I need more, Belle! What happened? Tell me what happened, Belle. Sit down at the table. Start at the beginning. Give me details. What precisely is wrong here?"

He poured them both a cup of coffee from the stove and snatched a pan of uncut bread from the counter before he sat down by her. Maybe it would help if he asked questions to get her started. "Now, where are Sari and Mary Ann?"

"Sari is in the nursery sleeping, but Mary, oh, Grey, Mary's not anywhere on the ranch. It's what I'm trying to tell you. She's not here. She disappeared into thin air Monday morning in the rain before the norther hit. Someone took her!"

The front door opened, and JD was drawn to the kitchen by the commotion. He took in the stricken faces. Without saying a word, he poured himself a cup of coffee and grabbed a chunk of the bread leaning against the counter woofing it down. He stood there waiting to be brought up to speed. They both just sat staring in shock at him, even Grey. When neither spoke soon enough to suit him, JD became all business and spoke with a commanding authority.

"I saw one of your men on the rise watching over the house. There doesn't seem to be anyone else around, except you, Belle. Where is everyone? When I was brushing and feeding the horses, I noticed some things out of place. There's been a struggle in the barn apparently. Who was fighting, Belle? What was it about?"

Grey said, "Mary Ann's gone. Sari's upstairs asleep. It's all I've been able to understand. She's gonna tell us the rest of it, calmly, the whole story, Belle."

Both men continued eating hunks of the warm bread while waiting on Belle to start talking. Her face was red and puffy from crying. Applying pressure wasn't going to help. Their eyes never left her face while more than half of the bread disappeared quickly. They hadn't eaten since cold biscuits and bacon in the saddle this morning.

"It was a few days after you rode out, Grey. It was washday, and it was a while before Coley, and I noticed Mary Ann wasn't in the house. She usually sleeps until Sari's second feeding, so I didn't check on her. Sari started crying and didn't stop. Coley was upstairs searching Wisteria's room, and we met in the nursery. Mary always answers Sari's cries. I opened the door to her bedroom. Everything seemed in order except for, no Mary. We looked for her upstairs first and then downstairs. Coley searched outside.

"Mary Ann had just vanished! Coley looked around outside while I tended Sari. He found nothing but what you saw in the barn, JD. He rang the alarm on the back porch. I can't get the sound of it out of my head! Smith got here first and looked at the scene of the scuffle. He recognized Mary's shoe prints. There were lots of boot prints that all matched, but he has no idea who was with her. There was a note she'd dropped. It was from you, Grey, something you'd written to Mary. There was blood, a patch of blood on the hay littering the barn floor."

Grey's breath hitched.

"There was a tight wad of dirty rag nearby like one that might be used to gag someone. Pegasus was gone too, and Sunny was badly hurt in the struggle. He hardly ever left her side, you know. He'd lost blood. Cookie stitched him. His ribs were tender, but none were broken. He stayed at the bunkhouse, so Cook was handy to tend him, but a couple of days ago he ran off. Nobody has seen hide nor hair of Sunshine since then. Your brothers think he might be out looking for Mary Ann.

"The few hoof prints Smith found indicated Pegasus is carrying a light load, so Mary was riding him. The other horse's prints weren't recognizable as belonging to any of our ranch horses. The tracks were deeper, like carrying a much heavier rider. It was raining and blowing most of the day. There was not much of a trail left to follow. One of Mary's shoes was found by the gate. Poor Mary didn't take her shawl or bonnet, and she's only wearing one shoe! The norther brought cold wind and rain. The cold has never left.

"I've been staying here in the house with Sari, baking bread and cookies to help Cookie keep everyone fed. Colby's been here to protect us and watch over the house and barns. Smith and our men go out every day to search while a few are left to work the ranch. Smith said not to worry if he wasn't home tonight, because he was planning to ride farther east than anyone's looked yet."

"On the second day a hidden cold camp was found. Someone had been watching the house. It was littered with empty bean cans, whiskey bottles, and trash. Smith and Coley saw signs of only one man. They found where his horse had been tied up behind the rocks. They found another note, but it doesn't say who received it or who wrote it. The wind had blown it into a bush, and it got hung up in the tangles.

"The sheriff came with men to help, but they didn't stay long. The sheriff said there wasn't any use to keep looking. He said his bet is she's probably been taken across the New Mexico border to be sold. You know how surly and worthless the town sheriff is!"

JD and Grey agreed with her.

"Smith listened to the coot until he'd heard enough and exploded in anger. Quick as lightening, he punched the sheriff in the nose. He may have broken it. The sheriff was bleeding like a stuck hog. He yelled at Smith and told him to call off the search. Some of the boys held Smith back, or he would have pulled him off his horse before he could leave.

"Cookie is out in the bunkhouse. The hands are doing the necessities to keep the ranch going. We're shorthanded. Every man is ready to do anything needed, but there aren't enough men, Grey. Smith keeps track of places looked at already, and he's run out of places. Smith told the hands their loyalty wouldn't be forgotten, and there were bonuses coming."

"Where are the notes you mentioned, Belle?" Grey asked.

"I have them right here. I didn't know Mary had the note from you. She's been awfully depressed you left, Grey. She never mentioned anything about a note from you."

Belle retrieved the two papers from the China cabinet and handed one of them to Grey. His face was solemn as he read what he'd written to Mary. She meant more to Grey than these clipped words. He stared out the window for a minute. JD and Belle remained quiet, giving him time to process his thoughts.

"Reading what I wrote now, I see only abrupt and impersonal words written to a girl who means so much more to me. From the condition of the paper, she had studied what I'd written a lot. She deserved a lot more from me than this. After I went to her room before bed Sunday night, we talked and got close. I enjoyed our time together, and I think she did too. I'm in love with her, and she doesn't know."

Belle handed him the second note. "This one came from the cold camp."

Lay low. Don't come back here.
Use money to stay away.

JD read over Grey's shoulder and let out a long, low whistle. "This person was getting paid to kidnap Mary, but it doesn't tell us much else. What would anyone have to gain?" JD asked almost to himself.

Grey looked at Belle and asked, "Belle, what did you think when you first saw this piece of paper?"

"I didn't have to think. It was written by Wisteria, of course. I recognized her handwriting immediately. She might as well have signed her name."

"JD, Belle's right. Wisteria wrote this. Wisteria threw threats around like a knife thrower last Sunday. She's the one behind this, no doubt in my mind. She made it clear on Sunday afternoon she wanted Mary Ann gone."

"This isn't enough by itself," JD said. "If this note matches samples of Wisteria's handwriting, it can be entered into court as evidence to consider. However, she doesn't admit to anything. It's only circumstantial evidence. A good lawyer, and she will have the best, will overemphasize the point to a judge and jury.

"Something else incriminating and more direct, or a witness, must be brought forward. Alone, this isn't worth the paper used to write it. No matter how bad the words look, it's not enough to convict her of kidnapping. It does, though, show a link from the author to the actual kidnapper."

Coley had come in while they were talking. He, Grey, and JD decided the ill-mannered sheriff's suggestion Mary might be at the New Mexico border was a notion worth following. It was painful to imagine Mary's kidnapper was selling her to Comancheros. Any woman sold to them ends up a captive of the Comanches.

Grey and JD discussed riding west toward the border and then turning northwest to follow it toward Portales, New Mexico. It was a sobering fact the Comancheros were dealing in human flesh with the Comanches. They rendezvoused with the Mexicans to make the exchanges along the border with one foot in Texas and the other foot in New Mexico. After the transactions were made, the captives would be taken by the Comanches who bought them never to be seen again.

The men who did business with the Comancheros were as vile as the Comancheros themselves. Selling flesh was an abomination to God. Being taken to a Comanche village could be a worse fate than death. The men who rounded up women and children to sell to the Comancheros, knowing what could happen to them, had no conscience. It was the devil's work. Grey would have to get his wife back before or right after she crossed the border.

He jotted some information down and handed it to Coley.

"Take this to Cap Rock right away. Send a telegram to the captain. Maybe he can spare men to head in the direction I'm headed."

Belle gathered up food for them to take and a change of clothes for each. Coley saddled their mounts and filled four canteens for them with fresh water before he left for Cap Rock to send the telegram. The men had checked their weapons and over-stocked their stashes of ammunition. Grey was satisfied Spanish Flight was sound and good to go. He'd depended on the exceptional horse to save his life more than once.

At the last minute, Belle ran out of the house waving a coat and crying. "Here, take this! She doesn't even have her shawl or bonnet to keep her warm. You find her, Grey, JD, bring her home. You must do it. I'm not losing another sister-in-law."

CHAPTER 29

Mary Ann Byrd ✦

Mary Ann was shivering with the cold, and her body was stiff from being tied to Pegasus for so long. She felt as if her breasts might burst. They were ripe with milk and painfully swollen. The uncomfortable globes were growing tighter and firming up like melons. The weight on her chest and the stretching of her skin nagged at her nerves. The protruding nipples were dripping but not enough to relieve the steady ache building to a crescendo.

What was she supposed to do to ease this relentless, building pressure? Other women must have faced similar dilemmas, but they probably were not bound to horses. Squeezing the sore flesh between her upper arms didn't cause much, if any, but it did cause her to cry out. She was in misery. She knew it wasn't going to get better without nursing Sari. The thought of the baby girl going hungry when she had so much milk to give brought Mary Ann great sorrow and tears ran down her face making her colder.

She could smell Pa's whiskey. She never thought she'd be thanking God for the devil's whiskey! Her pa was a worthless drunk, and she had suffered the consequences of his vice with liquor all her life. Now, ironically, it might be the only thing she had going for her except for having Pegasus to depend on. His drinking might allow her a chance to get home.

She waited anxiously for this sorry excuse of a man to reach the point of passing out. She knew from experience it would be midmorning before his eyes opened again. By then, she and Pegasus could be long gone and out of his reach. This might be the only opportunity she'd get to make a run for freedom. She had to get loose. It would take some begging to convince him to untie her.

"Pa! Pa, I must go to the bushes because I can't hold my water any longer. Please untie me. I promise not to give you cause to be sorry. I'll do everything exactly as you say."

Once she was free of the restraints, she'd be the perfect prisoner until the opportunity came for her to slip away. She'd be so helpful around the camp; he'd not retie her. The horse made her feel not so powerless, but he also made her think of Sunny. Poor Sunshine had given his life trying to save hers. Pa killed him for his devotion. His death made her deeply sad. Sunny deserved tears to be shed for him, but she couldn't find the strength to mourn right now. Mary Ann was in too much trouble of her own and didn't have the extra grit to spare.

Laziness was one of Pa's many weaknesses. Reminding him of how useful she could be to him if she was untied was all the persuading he needed. He'd been sucking on his bottle periodically all day in the saddle and wasn't thinking straight. Allowing Mary Ann to walk about the camp and use her hands was a serious mistake.

"I've 'bout rode as fer as I want taday. I'll untie ya. Go yonder ta do yer bidness. Don't git outta my sight! Ya hear me? When yer done, come back 'n get us a fire goin', then heat some beans."

He tossed the saddle bag of grub at her feet.

"Stir a little jerky in them beans fer extry flavor an' add some brown sugar. I'm hungry. After we eat the victuals, we'll turn in 'til morn'n. Horses have to rest."

Mary Ann wasted no time in stiffly squatting where he'd sent her. She was mindful of snakes hiding in the grass. Snakes were everywhere in Texas along with stinging bugs, sharp goat heads, droughts, sandstorms, wild hogs, and cyclones. Sometimes she thought dangerous things in nature were created just to make people suffer. There was always plenty of suffering to go around from what she could see.

Mary had just struggled to her feet after finishing her business and only taken a couple of steps before a big furry whoosh knocked her down. She panicked and screamed because at first, she thought she'd been jumped by a wolf. To be eaten by a wolf would be a horrible way to go. Before she could make sense of what was happening, a big tongue commenced to licking her whole face. Then she threw her sore arms around Sunshine in recognition, and now she found the tears she hadn't shed for him before.

Oh, Sunshine!

BB heard the commotion and started cursing loudly. "Tha' damn, blasted dog, thought I'd kilt 'im this mornin'. If he keeps followin', I'll sell him to the Comanches too. They'll either need 'em or eat 'em!" He laughed at the cruel joke he'd made at the yellow hound's expense.

After Sunny settled down and Pa went back to drinking, she used the torn bodice of her dress to tear strips and then tied them together. She wound the long strip around her chest several times binding her breasts securely to her torso. The tight wrapping minimized the stress of their heavy weight and kept them from bouncing. Mary was starving, and Pa didn't have to remind her again about the beans. He did keep on ranting about other grievances, but she barely heard his continuous haranguing as she worked.

She was ravenous and had to admit the sweet, hot beans and jerky tasted plenty good. She let Sunny have her bowl with a few beans held back for him. He licked it clean. Mary Ann hugged him close and buried her face in his thick fur. Now she had both Pegasus and her dog to give her courage. They'd be better off at the ranch, but she was thankful both were here with her.

"Pa, what did you mean about, if Sunny keeps following, you'll sell him to the Comanches too? What are you planning, Pa?"

"I'm takin' ya to meet up with Comancheros. We've been angling northwest for a couple of hours. They'll be waitin' on tha New Mexico line. They buy all the females and children they can find, and trade 'em to tha Comanches fer money, hides, leatherwork er whatever they can git. It's how they make their livin'.

"Tha Comanches are crazy to get hands on fresh women and children. They keep 'em fer theirselves as slaves, er wives, er trade 'em off to other Injuns. I'm sure I kin get somethin' fer the big dog and more fer the white horse."

She turned her back on Pa and pretended she was planning to sleep. She wouldn't let him see the sheer terror on her face. He didn't deserve the satisfaction of knowing how afraid she was. Long ago, she'd quit asking herself what she'd done to have to suffer so much on this earth. Finally, she'd realized the answer was nothing. She'd done nothing to earn the torment she'd lived through. The baby she carried, Sari, and Grey were the only joys she'd ever known. If only for a brief time, she'd had happiness. Pegasus and the dog were bonuses.

If Grey knew where she was, he'd come rescue her. Mary Ann believed this in her heart to be a fact. His brothers would have figured out by now she'd been taken from the ranch, but they wouldn't know who took her. Grey would have no idea where to start looking. If he's not home yet, he still thinks she's on the ranch right where he left her. She's on her own to get out of this fix. She was used to being on her own. She'd take Pegasus and Sunny and leave Pa far behind.

She could do this!

CHAPTER 30

Nacona ◆

Nacona rode off by himself today. He felt the need to be alone with his thoughts. His Comanche name translated into, One Who Wanders. This title allowed him many privileges and freedoms other braves didn't have. His grandmother was a seer, a person with supernatural insight into the future. She was remembered and revered as a prophet. It was said she still watched over them in spirit through her grandson.

She'd named him well because it was believed he had the ability to disappear and reappear at will. To some extent they were right. He could come and go as he pleased and disappear for extended periods of time. None of the people dared to question his movements. Whenever he magically materialized to walk among the people again, he was venerated for the intuitive wisdoms and predictions he shared. It was assumed his grandmother, Topsannah, always rode with him. They said he walked with his grandmother in the afterlife and witnessed the future through her eyes.

Nacona rode by himself often to escape the commotion

and ignorance of his brothers. The braves reminded him of squirrels jumping from one limb to another and always picking fights and chattering like children. Constantly there was boisterous arguing, roughhousing, and flinging of themselves bodily into each other. Everything they did resulted in noise, blows, and brawls. Comanche men were born fighters, and the young braves were always practicing, training for the next fight. They could not focus long enough to contemplate the bigger picture of the future.

Nacona couldn't bear this human stew of constant chaos. The consequences of their short sightedness were shown in the steadily declining population of the people. Entire bands were being wiped out by guns, starvation, and disease. Lack of attention and organization would be the ruination and downfall of the Comanche Nation. After the Civil War, Grant started annihilating them systematically, and they were too naive to realize what was happening. Grant had learned much from experiences in fighting and winning the Civil War. He was now using the knowledge in a merciless, deadly battle against their existence. They weren't focused enough to strategize their retaliations.

The scream of a woman led him to the top of a rise with the vantage point to see into the shallow valley below. A large yellow dog had a white woman down on the ground, but they were interacting like friends, not scuffling like enemies. Regardless of size difference, the dog posed no threat. Her scream had quickly turned into laughter. If running water had a laugh, he imagined it would sound like the crystal-clear quality of her laughter. He couldn't peel his eyes away from the girl with the long, golden-brown hair. He was too far away to make out features well, but the wind was carrying her spirit, and he confusingly recognized the essence of two separate souls. He thought he recognized one of them.

She stopped laughing and stood abruptly when a man waving a bottle and shouting angrily approached. His large bulk towered over her small frame. The dog challenged his menacing dominance. The man kicked at the animal, but he backed off when the girl yelled out for him to stop. At the same time, she put herself between the man and the dog. It was a bold move for such a small lass. The man was a behemoth in comparison.

Her head was bobbing, and she was talking angrily. Nacona could only catch a word or two. The man was now yelling at her and the dog both. She had her legs slightly spread in a stance showing courage and strength. She was postured to defend the animal even though the man could break her in two like a stick. She was a banty rooster facing a coyote. This one had the heart of a Comanche Warrior Woman. Nacona admired her bravery, but knew she'd never win the battle if she had to fight alone. This oaf of a man standing in her way was only a part of what she was facing.

Using the scrubby trees and brush as cover, Nacona had gradually been inching closer. He hadn't recognized the girl's identity at first. He'd never forget this man though, a son of a dog. He gambled away his daughter to three outlaws, this very girl, in a card game rigged against him. He was drunk and had easily been swindled to hand her over to avoid paying a price with his own skin. This white man was worse than a coward. Nacona knew his character because he'd been one of the three outlaws who'd tricked him.

He was Frank McGill then, all dressed sharply in black, wearing guns and a big hat. It was from a time when he was running with bad men and living outside the law. His skin was the light color of baked bread, and he had a thick head of brown wavy hair to match. Frank could pass easily for a white man or an Indian. His well to do Irish father made sure he was educated and spoke eloquently. He was well-read, could write, and knew numbers better than most. Frank had a sizeable inheritance sitting in a Texas bank under an alias name. He wasn't a poor man by any means.

Under Topsannah's tutelage, he understood the culture

and was fluent in the Comanche language. The Comanches had no written linguistics or government, but he learned the chain of command and how to leave messages through secret signs. Nacona was conditioned physically and mentally as a child to run many miles without stopping. He'd developed strong, lean muscles, and perfected the habits and skills of a warrior. He could ride a horse in many positions at many speeds without a saddle.

He'd observed the girl with the big white stallion and knew she shared a close kinship with her horse. He watched as she talked to the proud beast and exchanged breath through his nose. The horse, yellow dog, and she clearly belonged together as one. She stole glances at her pa many times, watching nervously, always watching for something. When the old man finally passed out cold from the liquor, the trio silently made their break for freedom.

She'd die in this dangerous wilderness without support. If the Comancheros didn't find her, his Comanche brothers would. Nacona would help her get back home safely, but he had a proportionate trade for saving her life in mind. It had come to him in an omen he could not grasp the meaning of until now. He knew exactly why fate brought them back together again. The virgin he'd lain with in private was now increasing with his infant.

This woman rode hard, further demonstrating grit and determination along with the courage she'd already shown. She pushed the stallion hard into the night and expected the yellow dog to follow. Nacona let her have her lead until she veered dangerously close to his people. If she was taken by them, he'd have to fight a brother to the death to get her back. He closed in to overtake her.

Mary Ann Byrd ✦

Mary Ann didn't know north from south or east from west in this darkness. When the sun came up, she'd get her bearings. She needed to be going southeast in the general direction of the ranch. She and her animals required rest and water soon. She had no idea how long a horse could go without water. The horse must graze too. Mary saw a tree line in the distance. She'd stop when she reached it.

Her breasts were engorged and sore. Bouncing on the horse was agony even though she'd bound them earlier. She squeezed milk out as she was able, but it was nowhere near enough to give significant relief. She fretted over Sari not having the nourishment but riding toward home was the best she could do. Her mind was playing tricks on her. She was so terrified and tired, she was hallucinating. She heard and saw Pa, Comancheros, Comanches, and wild animals seeming to come at her from every direction.

An animal barreled out of nowhere and hit her horse from the side. She heard the cry of an Indian. If this wasn't really happening, then why would Sunny be growling and barking in the distance? The two horses squalled and both reared, pawing at the sky. The impact almost knocked her out of the saddle. She instinctively grabbed the pummel tightly with both hands and pulled against it to right herself. She instinctively leaned her upper body toward Pegasus's head until her cheek met his lathered neck. Her heels dug into the stirrups to brace herself. She tightened her calves in a spontaneous reaction.

Only by the skin of her teeth was she able to keep from sliding down Pegasus's back to the ground as his front hoofs reached high into the sky several times. The horses screamed and It seemed like he stood straight up on his hind legs for a full minute. In truth, the whole episode happened so fast she didn't have time to think lucidly. For a girl who'd never ridden much until she got to Byrd Ranch, managing to stay on Pegasus was an amazing feat she never wanted to repeat.

She'd lost the reins initially and couldn't keep Pegasus from finishing in a flat-out run as he fled to escape the melee. The marauding horse ran just as fast keeping up with

Pegasus. This couldn't get any worse until she saw an Indian now held his reins and was reaching out to grip the bridle. Once Pegasus was brought under control, the Indian reached one sinewy arm out, snatching her off onto his horse with him. There was no saddle, and she scrambled to get a fist full of the coarse mane, wrapping it around her hands. Mary was so overwhelmed. It hadn't occurred to her she'd been captured again.

Everything happening to her since Pa showed up at Byrd Ranch was a nightmare. She hollered, kicked, hit with her fists, twisted, grabbed, and yelled profanities she'd never used before. Then she cried and wailed. Nacona held on to her. He was surprised she was able to put up such an impressive fight. She made so much commotion for such a little one, but he couldn't blame her for making the effort. What did she think she could do against him? He held her close to his body until she drained her energy. He spoke into her ear using a stern voice.

"Close your mouth! Calm yourself, and I'll let go of you."

"You'll let me go?"

"No! I'll let go of you, but I will not let you leave."

He had her attention. She settled but then started sobbing uncontrollably. Again, he waited for the storm to roll over. Words would be wasted on a hysterical woman. She had a lot to cry out after all she'd been through. She had to know her pa was taking her to the flesh peddlers, and it would be a dreadful fate.

Nacona's intention was never to hurt her. He hadn't even caused pain the day the outlaws took her. Coupling was a natural act occurring between males and females. It didn't count as torture. Comanche men were dominant, and Comanche women submitted to them. It was a natural course of life. White culture was confusing and muddied the waters when it came to sex. Morals and a whole array of nonsense mixed and made up the rules of civilized society in such matters. He much preferred the simple thinking of saloon birds to the proper ladies in white society.

Nacona's aim now was only to stop her from angling farther north. She was getting too close to Comanche territory. It would not end well. Comanche men and women would delight in tormenting and disfiguring her. He wouldn't let it happen.

She was using one hand to wipe at her tears and the other to cradle her chest. "Cigala, are you hurt? Let me see." He knocked her hand away from the wrapping protecting her chest and replaced it with his flat palm. When he pressed against her full firm breasts, she cried out. He did it again and received the same response. Her breasts were engorged, tightly and were wet!

"What is wrong with you little one? Are you nursing?"

"I was when Pa stole me, but now I just hurt, really hurt! You're, wait, you're speaking, and I can understand you. We understand each other! How is this possible?"

"I'm not a common Comanche brave. My name is Nacona, and I am a breed. I was raised by my father, Franklin McGill, who was also a breed. He was a man of business, and I grew up in his house. I was educated in the white man's world, but my Comanche grandmother made sure I realized my Comanche roots as well.

"Cigala, you have nothing to fear from me. I will even protect you from my brothers if the need arises. We've met before, the two of us. You don't remember. Where is this baby you nurse?"

"Why do you call me, Cigala? My name is Mary Ann Byrd. What does the word you keep saying mean?"

"I gave you the name, Cigala, the first time I saw you. It means, Little One. Finding you here in the tall grass was fortuitous, but I saw you coming in a dream I did not comprehend so it is not entirely unexpected you are here."

Mary Ann didn't know what he was talking about. "What do you mean the first time you saw me? I've never seen you before!"

"It is not surprising you don't remember me. Your mind had shut down, and I was very different then, anyway. It is confusing. Tell me about this baby you're nursing. How old is it? Wherever is the baby now? How did you come to be here this night?"

"I'm nursing my husband's baby girl. Her real mother died in childbirth a month ago. It's complicated, but without the baby to nurse, my breasts have swollen with the milk. They're painful, and I don't know what to do. I'm miserable and getting worse. I think I'm running a fever.

"My pa is a very bad man, the worst. He despises me and is cruel. He took me in the dark away from my husband's home, but I'm running from him now. My man is kind, and we live on his ranch with his family. We haven't been married long. Things are good for me there, and I want to get back to him. I am carrying a child, but this baby is not his. Since his wife died, he had to have me to nurse his baby girl, and I needed a man to claim me and the baby growing inside. We married each other in a bargain, but I care for him very much. I am homesick and scared.

"Pa was planning to sell me, Pegasus, and Sunshine. I fear Pa will find us. He'll do anything for money, and he cares nothing for me. If I don't keep moving, my life will be over just when I have a chance for something good. No one knows who took me or where to find me. Maybe, they think I ran away from the ranch, but I hope not. I must get back, and I'm begging you to turn me loose."

"Quiet! Leaving me would be unwise. I will not allow your trash of a father to take you again. He will be the one to cry and beg this time. Don't be frightened of me! I won't let you get close to a Comanchero. Comanches, maybe, but I'll not allow them to lay a hand on you. You're getting back to your home, Cigala. I think your man along with another is traveling this way for you now. I'll see to it they find you. It will cost you, though."

"What do you mean? What will it cost me? I have no

money."

"You will see. First, I must leave you here alone for a while.

"No, please, no!"

"I will make sure you and the animals are safe, but you must stay silent and well hidden. I will mark the hiding place with my sign. If my brothers happen upon you, they'll see it and know you're mine. They might startle you but will not touch what is mine. When I return, I will bring food, water, and something to relieve your heavy breasts. I will give you herbs to break your fever and help you sleep while I'm gone. You'll understand what you must do for me in time."

~

Grey and JD rode through the night, stopping only to rest the horses. No man could risk riding a horse to death in rough country. It could cost him his life. They chewed on jerky and drank sparingly from their canteens. Their point of destination was Mary Ann, and they only had a hunch of where she might be. They could easily miss her by one mile or a few, but still Grey and JD would keep riding ahead with resolve.

CHAPTER 31

Mary Ann Byrd ✦

Mary and the animals were hidden safely against the rocks in a small pocket with only one opening. Nacona had closed it in with brush. It would be difficult to detect them there. The sunlight getting through was minimal. After a time, the herbs caused Mary's eyes to become heavy with a paralyzing fatigue. She jerked herself awake once but slipped back into oblivion. In the back of her mind, she knew staying awake was important because being alert might save her life. She could not keep her eyes open though. It was a foolish to try and fight sleep when she had no weapon and so little strength to defend herself. Swiftly a deep sleep thankfully overtook her.

She dreamed about Grey, and in her dream, he was holding her. She dreamed about Sari, the solemn Comanche, and the fearsome sight of him. She felt herself running free with Pegasus and Sunny. She believed Grey was coming to get her. Behind the mask of sleep, hidden in her dreams, there were no threats, no fear, no stress, no hunger, or pain. She was safe, sound, and on her way home already.

Seeing Nacona in early morning light, was unnerving. She had not imagined the wild look of an Indian, his fierce demeanor, or the contradictions in who she envisioned he was in the dark. She'd pictured him with straight black hair, not the russet color with a hint of a wave. The delicate, light coffee and cream shade of his skin was stunning. Indeed, he would easily pass for a white man with the right clothing. His arms and legs were taunt and well-defined with muscles. Veins like cords ran below the skin of his forearms. He was masculine and built well like she imagined a Greek God in the myths might be.

His dress was totally immodest. Nacona wore scant attire, yet he moved unashamedly and comfortably. Mary wanted to look away but was so fascinated she stared instead. Nacona wore a leather belt, of sorts, around his lean waist. A long, rectangular piece of leather looped between his legs with one end tucked under the belt in front and the other end tucked under it in the back to secure it in place covering his privates. He was naked from the waist up. A sizable knife with a deer horn handle stuck in a leather sheath riding his hips.

His legs were protected by loose fitting, deerskin leggings like a cowboy's chaps. High-topped moccasins were tied to his feet with leather thongs around his ankles. The caps of his shoes were made of soft, buttery deerskin. The soles were thicker and tougher leather, maybe buffalo. Small beads were sewn into the tops in a planned design. There was a riot of leather fringe making the moccasins most remarkable.

Black and white lines resembling lightning strikes were painted boldly on his face. Bright yellow circles were painted around his eyes. Shells hung from his earlobes, and a strand of them hung around his neck. A small bag was attached. A wide copper band circled one of his upper arms.

Even his spotted horse had been painted. There were yellow rings around his eyes, and white lightning bolts on his body. A bag of arrows, a bow, and a bladder of water were secured to the horse. There was no saddle, only a blanket. Every detail of Nacona and his horse was gregarious. Mary might have died from terror had she been able to see him well in the dark of night. It was better she hadn't. She wasn't afraid of him now, or at least, she tried not to be. Reason told her if he intended to hurt her, he would already have done so.

When he rode away, she'd felt isolated, uneasy, and alone when the strange-looking brave disappeared. He'd told her to use the time to rest and to not be afraid. He said he marked this place with a sign protecting her from his Comanche brothers. Whatever his sign was, she had to wonder if they would honor it. She was homesick and wanted with all her heart to return to Byrd Ranch. This very articulate man who used words sparingly and spoke directly to the point, was offering her a way back to Grey and Sari. He said Grey and another man were already on their way to find her. She had to believe Nacona's word was his bond. He would be coming back soon to take her home. She had no choice but to wait and see what the cost he indicated would be.

Through the sticks of brush, she could see the yellow rays of the sun rising higher in the sky. They were blasting heat and shining light upon the prairie grass. The slightest noise caused Mary Ann's heart to beat so fast, she could hardly catch the next breath. Her weepy breasts were still aching, but the fever had broken. She still needed the pressure of the milk released. She gave into lying down again and closing her eyes. It was just supposed to be for only a moment.

She dreamed of a baby crying, but the sound was nothing like Sari's cry. It was different, stronger, and more intense. Mary Ann awoke with a start. Disoriented memories of the nursery and her bedroom mixed with images of the present reality swam together in her head. Instead of a soft bed, the ground was hard. Instead of the smell of lilac soap, she was bombarded by the odors of soured milk and the musk of animals. Sunny was there licking her face soothingly, but a blinding light was hitting her along with the noise of branches being torn away. It caused her stomach to dip in dread until she recognized Nacona.

He was squatting in front of her with a real crying baby wrapped in a soft looking deerskin. This was the baby she had heard. It was unhappy and complaining. The brave held the bundle out to her. Without hesitation, she took it into her arms.

"He hungers. Feed him."

This was an order, not a statement, but she didn't hesitate to comply.

Nacona led Mary and the baby out into the air with Sunshine tagging behind. The baby boy had her mesmerized. He was like a doll with pudgy pink skin and red, curly hair. He smelled her dripping milk and rooted against her frantically searching to latch onto the source. She bared a breast for him immediately and offered a sore nipple. He took it greedily and she cried out when he sucked harder than she had expected, but the blessed relief trumped the pain. She gratefully smiled through it.

The Indian had returned from seeing to the animals and sat cross legged closely in front of her. He was staring intently as she fed, and the baby ate. She switched breasts when she felt the pressure of the swelling receding from the first one. He held out a small leather pouch to her.

"Herbs for the fever, take pinches several times until the fever leaves your body."

"Thank you. Tell me who this baby belongs to, Nacona."

"To you. He is your baby now. I am giving him to you. Take him."

"You can't just give a baby away. Won't his mother be looking for him? He's such a perfect little baby. You can't just hand him to me. I can't take someone else's baby home with me."

"His mother died in a battle, but I sired him, so he is mine to do with as I please. He looks more Irish than Comanche.

He will fit in with your world better than this one. I called his mother, Ava. It's an Irish name, Aoife, and it means beauty. She was a great woman warrior and died with much honor. Your bravery reminds me of her. Women in the village have been taking turns nursing him, but I wish him to have a mother and a safe home.

"Resources supporting the life of the Comanche Nation grow smaller every day. Buffalo are scarce because the soldiers are paying for white men to kill them off. They leave the meat to rot on the ground after the hides have been taken. Soon the soldiers will come to push the Comanche people, like cattle, to a reservation. I do not wish him to stay here for what is to come. He will die. I want him to live well and prosper.

"Taking this boy as yours is the price you must pay to get home, Cigala. I don't want him to be here any longer. Look at him. Does he look like a Comanche to you? This is my son, and he bears the look of my mixed heritage. I am choosing for him to walk in the white man's world with you. Sometime back I had a vision of two brothers growing together sharing one mother. In the future, I saw a cowboy, a strong father, teaching them to become impressive men of great depth, leaders.

"This boy's name is Etuhassun. It means Sunstone. Hide it in your heart for him always but give him a new name to serve him better. He needs one to fit into the white man's world. It must be a strong, solid name. He will grow up on the ranch you love and with the people you trust."

"And you, what is to become of you? Go with us. Get away from here."

"I cannot leave with you, Cigala. There are so many reasons. I am still considering where I will be when the soldiers come. I have not decided yet, but I will do what I can for Grandmother's people until then. Their window in time is closing.

"Are you ready?"

"Ready for what, Nacona?"

"Are you ready to go home? I sent some of my brothers scouting. They saw two men on horses headed this way. One rides a black, and the other rides an appaloosa. These are no doubt your people."

"Yes! Yes, I know those horses! They got here fast!"

"Both are very brave men to come. They hold you in high esteem. Which is your man?"

"He rides the appaloosa. My husband's name is Greyson Byrd."

"Let us go then. I will take you to them." Nacona didn't mention he'd sent the scouts on to find and torment the old drunk to his death. By now, her pa was minus his balls and other various body parts. The Comanches took pride in killing slowly. This dishonorable man, BB Barton, had caused Cigala misery for the last time.

Mary Ann didn't know if she wanted to laugh or cry first when she heard Grey, and JD were coming for her. She couldn't control the tears falling, but neither could she stop laughing. Like a crazy person, she did both actions together at once. Nacona brought her to a rise so she could know for sure Grey was on his way. She'd never been this fortunate or this happy. Seeing Grey and JD in the far distance filled her with joy.

Nacona's spotted horse stood a little behind Pegasus. Etuhassun was cradled to her and sleeping. She'd decided on a name for him.

"Nacona," she called out. "I will call your son Stone. Is it a name to your liking?"

She waited for an answer, but one never came. Perhaps he couldn't hear her words above the brushing sound of the tall sea of grass moving in the wind. She turned Pegasus around to say the new name again, but Nacona was gone. He'd evaporated into the air or so it seemed.

She spoke aloud to him anyway. "Stone Byrd it is, but I will write Etuhassun in my heart forever and someday tell him of his beautiful warrior mother, Aoife. I will not forget to tell him of his Irish Indian father, Nacona, when he is old enough to understand. His heritage will not be lost to him."

It saddened her to think he hadn't touched his child one last time or said goodbye. It seemed so heartbreaking until the truth came to her. Nacona loved Stone so much he'd made the greatest sacrifice a father can make. This mysterious man gave his son over to a better life and rode away. He'd given him up to save him from what was to come. No amount of parting words and final touches could measure up to equal such a gift of this magnitude.

Goodbye, Nacona, and thank you.

CHAPTER 32

━━━◆◆◦❖◦◆◆━━━

Greyson Byrd ◆

Spanish Flight ate up mile after mile with Grey urging him forward. Praying fervently, Grey had faith God would lead JD and him to Mary in this great, expanse of swaying prairie. God was the only hope of intersecting with Mary Ann's location. Every instinct was telling him to keep going and not give up on finding his wife before it was too late. He ached for the opportunity to tell her everything in his heart. He should have said it on Sunday night instead of missing the chance. He'd boldly proclaim his love for her when they reunited.

JD, riding along beside him on Newman, was the best friend he'd ever had. Their paths had first crossed in the line of duty. He'd proved over and over to be a cunning and fearless lawman. They'd had each other's backs from the beginning of their acquaintance. Grey was feeling contrite for possibly leading his friend right into the hands of Comanches. It was conceivable they might both die a wicked death before the day was over.

There was no guarantee Mary Ann wasn't already dead

or moved to a place far beyond their reach, but as long as he was still breathing, he'd keep searching. Something told him, deep inside of himself, she was alive and waiting for him. The leather of JD's saddle creaked as he stood up in the stirrups to get a better look at something catching his attention. Grey followed his line of vision to the northwest. JD was pointing a finger directing Grey to follow his line of vision.

"Look yonder along the ridge at the crest of the rise. What do you see? I can't quite make it out?"

Grey pulled his spyglass out of the saddle bag and put it to his eye.

"I see it, JD, but too far away to make it out, could be a Comanche. We'd stand a chance against one or two, but where there's one, there are usually many more. I apologize ole friend for leading you into the backyard of deadly danger. Maybe it's not too late for you to turn around and go back the way we came. I have to do this, but I wouldn't blame you a bit for pulling out."

"Oh, no, my friend, I'm right where I choose to be. I'd be trying to help Mary with or without you. Mary Ann Byrd is my friend. Being here is my own idea. She's had too hard a life, and I want her back and safe with you on Byrd Ranch with Sari. We won't give up partner. Something tells me there's a good chance we're going to find her alive, by golly. She'll be going home with us when this is over."

They rode ahead in silence. They were alert and aware of every sound around them. JD kept surveilling the perimeters, hunting for the slightest change or glimpse of movement. Grey kept eyes on the ridge still too far away to determine what they might be riding into. Unfastening the straps holding the pistols securely in leather holsters, both men twirled cylinders, checking the readiness of their handguns.

Between the two of them, there were two rifles, two shotguns, four handguns, two Bowie knives and each had a smaller knife tucked in a boot. The rifles were for distance, the shotguns for closer range, the handguns for face-to-face, and the knives for hand-to-hand. Their double bullet belts crossed in the middle of their chest and saddle bags held many more rounds of ammunition. Each had one of the rifles resting across his lap with the shotguns still in their scabbards. If need be, they'd fight like hell, and pray their efforts would be enough.

"Whatever it is on the ridge, JD, is on the move now and coming toward us. It's not moving fast. Do you see any signs of movement around us?"

"Nothing, Grey! I'm keeping my eyeballs peeled. All's quiet so far."

Salty perspiration ran into their eyes, making them burn and water. Drops of moisture rolled down their necks dampening bandanas. An aura of tension radiated around each man. Muscles were contracted tightly, and jaws were nervously clenching. Each man was silently talking to God Almighty reminding Him their souls were His.

The horses sensed the changes in the body languages of their riders. They became anxious and alert. They'd read these forewarnings of danger emanating from their men before. The strain of their riders became their strains as they worked together as disciplined teams. Each man and the horse he rode were one unit braced together against the imminent action pending. The horses' heads were held stiffened and high. Their hardened ropes of muscle were twitching under tension. Both blew powerful gusts of air in and out of their noses. Their internal hair triggers were set for signals from their masters to turn and run or charge and engage.

Mary Ann ✦

Mary Ann rode down the slope and slowly started toward Grey and JD. She was anxious to swallow up the distance between them, but sensed Comanche might be watching. She wanted to leave a wide gap between her and the Comanches as soon as possible, but common sense told her she was not free and clear yet. She vowed never to venture into their land again if she made it out today. Mary had not had one peaceful moment since being taken from Byrd Ranch. She'd rather die on Byrd land than leave it ever again. Pegasus was surefooted and stout. Stone was tied securely against her body, full and sleeping. Sunny followed, and she drew courage from his steady companionship.

Greyson Byrd ◆

Raising the spyglass to his eye once more, Grey could better see what was ahead but still in the distance. He wanted to shout out loud at what he saw, but he knew to make noise wouldn't be prudent. This was Comanche territory, and caution had to be the rule. They weren't out of danger yet and sudden noises or movement could cause chaos to reign. Mary Anne's Pegasus was in front, and there was Mary. Mary Ann was riding her Pegasus! Sunshine was following right behind them. He might have known Sunny would find his special person! Grey had been so fearful he might never see his wife again. He pulled Spanish Flight up short.

"They're there, JD! I swear it's them! Look!"

JD held the spyglass to his eye and started grinning from ear to ear.

"It sure is, Grey! I've never been so glad to see a parade in my life. What the hell has happened to them? Your dog may well have been dead, but he sure looks alive now. All three look to be healthy, sound as dollars, Grey. The odds have been stacked against them! We found Mary! We found her! I can't wait to hear her stories. She's one tough woman. You got a good one, Grey!"

The cowboys urged their mounts to continue forward.

Mary Ann was Grey's only focus. She was all he could think about. She'd kicked the big white stallion up a notch.

Sunny fell behind, but he was running was running with peeled back lips. He couldn't quite keep up. Mary Ann's golden-brown hair was flying behind her like a flag. She was a most beautiful sight to behold.

Sunny was barking. A baby was crying. Grey called to her, and she hollered back. He jumped from the appaloosa and ran to pull her into his arms. The reunion was a glorified, emotional celebration. Grey tried to hug Mary to him, but there was a baby in the way. He was awake and crying from the ruckus. Grey didn't let the bundle deter him. He stepped beside her. With one arm he held Mary Ann in his embrace. With his free hand he captured her chin and gently turned her head to the side tilting it until their mouths were aligned. He crushed his lips relentlessly to hers and kissed her like she had never dreamed a kiss could be. It was deep, long, and she kissed her husband right back.

"Mary Ann, I love you, my darlin'. I should have told you last Sunday night in your room because I knew then. It was foolish of me to put it off. Please forgive me for the short note I left. You dropped it in the barn. When I read it again, I was ashamed how terse the words sounded. I swear to love and cherish you forever. Forever, Mary Ann Byrd!"

Then he kissed her again just as urgently as before and then again and again until she was breathless.

"Grey, I love you and Sari too. I didn't know how much I loved you until we were separated. From the minute Pa took me off the ranch on Monday, I started trying to get back to you. I was so scared Grey! I had no idea you'd know where to look for me, but I didn't doubt you'd come if you could. How did you find me?"

"It's a long story, Sweetheart. Everyone on the ranch has been out searching for you. Mary, I don't understand whose baby this is, but neither do I really care. You have lots of time to explain all that's happened to you. Right now, you in my arms, is all I need.

"You and I are all this baby boy has in the world, Grey.

It's a long story to share. His name is Stone. I had to bring him with me. What else could I do? He couldn't be left to die. He wouldn't have a chance back there. I couldn't guarantee I could even get us home, but I was going to die trying. Pegasus and Sunny helped me. I had to see you and Sari again. I just had to make it back. I've been so worried about Sari. Surely there is room for one more on the ranch, Grey."

"Don't you worry, we're all on our way home together, our home. You did right in bringing him with you. I guess our little family of four is going to be a larger family of five! Little Stone will never know he was alone in this world, and it's the way it should be. He'll only know of love and family, his family. Let's get ourselves back where we belong, back on the ranch!

"We owe JD a great deal of credit for coming with me to get you! We'll never be able to repay him."

CHAPTER 33

Coley Byrd ✦

B ack at the ranch, Coley had emptied Wisteria's room bare of any of the woman's possessions. Only after thoroughly checking pockets, hems, linings, boxes, between book pages and toiletries did he bundle them all together. To do this, he stole bits of time around the intense responsibilities of keeping the ranch secure. Coley had been spread thin all week coordinating around-the-clock sentries, including himself. He had been making most of the routine sweeps.

The surface inspection of the bedroom produced printed information on herbs and other small items of interest. He confiscated these but they were nothing unusual considering Wisteria's fascination with the healing potential of herbs. The tin concealed under the feather bed did pique his interest. It contained hard discs of white lozenges garishly decorated in bright emerald swirls and three packets of powder. What appeared to be candy and tea weren't red flags, but where they were stashed seemed very strange. He'd have Doc take a look.

Coley fully intended to examine the room further. He'd look under any loose-fitting floorboards. Then he'd check for unstable wall panels, slits in the wallpaper, or for places something could be concealed. He was taking a buckboard this morning into Caprock with Wisteria's personal things and delivering them to her place.

Coley knew little about the woman or what she did when she wasn't underfoot at the ranch. He'd never once cared to know. Delivering her things as a courtesy was a good excuse for him to get an overview of her property while making a personal contact. The cagey woman had to be approached with caution. He couldn't afford to underestimate her.

Grey's captain sent someone with experience to work beside him. He had already arrived. The sheriff wouldn't know the new man in town was a Texas Ranger or about any suspicions the Byrd brothers had. As a lawman, Walter was just a badge pinned on a sleeping dog drawing pay and breathing. Wisteria owned interests in Cap Rock and probably him as well. He couldn't be trusted.

Luke, the undercover ranger, had already paid a visit to Coley at the ranch. They devised a plan involving Coley getting closer to Wisteria. Know your friends but know your enemies better was the key to their strategy. They would keep their eyes on her, ears open, and dig inside and outside of her businesses and properties. She'd be under surveillance until enough incriminating evidence could be ferreted out to make a solid arrest.

Before his sister-in-law, Mary Ann, vanished, Coley was only interested in connecting Wisteria to Beth's death. Now, the unsigned note from the kidnapper's cold camp needed to be linked tighter to her as well. He also needed the name of the person receiving it.

Coley pulled the rig around to the back door of Wisteria's two-story house on the edge of town. There were no neighbors within shouting distance, so she had plenty of privacy. He'd never been here before and took in what he could see from where he was perched on the buckboard. The barn was well-kept, and the double doors were chained shut with a heavy padlock. On a back corner of the property was a high, solid wooden fence much taller than a man could see over. Its gate was also secured like the doors on the barn. He was fascinated by the possible hidden secrets guarded by the locks.

Wisteria, old girl, what are you hiding?

He was glad to see her little buggy mare nibbling grass in a spacious side paddock where there was a small shelter from the weather, a food box, and a water trough. The horse was leisurely swatting away flies with its tail. Coley was glad to see it well tended.

Knocking on the back door, he waited hat in hand. The curtain fluttered and Wisteria peered out. An overly enthusiastic smile spread across her face in recognition. The sound of the inside lock chain being slid across the latch was followed by the door being opened wide. Wisteria gushed over him, and he awkwardly responded in kind to the unexpected friendly reception.

"Coley? What a surprise! What are you doing here? I don't think you've ever come to see me before. Come in."

"No, Ma'am, I've never been here. This is a nice piece of property."

The fact was they really didn't know each other, but he'd gladly play along with the ruse. He'd always avoided speaking to her or even being in the same room with her if he could avoid it. He'd resented Wisteria invading his home. When Grey officially kicked her off the ranch a week ago, he'd felt a burden being lifted. She was an interloper, only there because Beth allowed it. Give Wisteria an inch and she'd take a mile. Coley couldn't stand her.

"Miss Wisteria, I'm delivering your personal things from the ranch. We've been doing some house cleaning and organizing since Beth died. I was coming into town anyway, and it seemed a good time to bring them to you."

"Oh, how very thoughtful, Coley. You've always been sweeter than your two brothers. I'm quite saddened by the rift caused on Sunday. Beth was my only family, and now I only have Sari. You know, my cousin loved me dearly. We were as close as sisters. She wouldn't approve of Grey saying the things he did and then pushing me away. You, Coley, are a gracious gentleman. You're a peacemaker! Beth would be so proud of you."

"Yes, Ma'am, I expect you're right about Beth, but don't think too hard of Grey. Suddenly losing Beth hit him mighty hard and then Sari almost dying was just too much all at once. He'll come around, but we'll all have to be patient until then."

"Mmmm, around town the word is his little friend has up and run off. I wasn't a bit surprised to hear it. Now if y'all could only get rid of Belle so easily, there might be hope for the Byrd brothers yet."

Coley recoiled inside from the lash of Wisteria's harsh tongue. He maintained a smile and was careful not to reflect his own opinion. What he really wanted to do was dump her belongings in the yard and retreat, but the conversation had to be kept sociable, if it was to be productive.

"I'm sure Smith would not agree, Miss Wisteria." He smiled crisply.

"Where do you want me to put these bundles? I'll carry them inside for you."

"How kind of you, Coley. Please put them in the dining room. I'll sort through and put everything away from there. I'm sure many items will be rerouted to the church's poor box.

"I won't deny I hadn't even considered Grey would close the room at the ranch to me. It's been like my second home these last four years. I was so looking forward to being there and helping Beth's sweet baby."

Yeah, like you helped her mama.

"Go ahead and get started. I'll make a tray of lemonade

and cookies for us to enjoy in the parlor when you're done. We can sit down and have a nice visit."

"I'm happy to bring the bundles inside for you, Ma'am, but I can't stay. I do thank you for offering refreshments, but we'll have to do it on another day. I have a long list of errands this morning and extraordinarily little time.

"I'm sorry Grey offended you. He was hasty in telling you not to come back to Byrd Ranch. It's going to take a while until he's thinking straight again. I'm sure he'll regret what he said to you and apologize in due time. I just thought you might as well have these things before he takes a notion to throw them out. He's a bit irrational right now."

"It's not your fault, Coley.

"Now, what about the girl? Has there been any word on her whereabouts yet?"

"No, it does look like she's gone for good. There's been no sign or word from her, and it looks like she won't be back. Lots of men have been looking for her, but the search is winding down now. There's no reason to keep beating a dead horse if she doesn't want to be found. It's best we all get on with our lives."

"Indeed, Coley! You have a good head on your shoulders. You've grown up to be a handsome, intelligent man."

This preliminary contact had run its course. All this snide talk made Coley want to empty his stomach, but he kept a stiff, frozen smile on his face instead. The moment all the packages were deposited into the dining room, he said his goodbye and left the premises. He'd seen what he needed to see, and he'd reached his quota of syrupy crap from Wisteria today. Besides, there was sure as hell no way he'd stick around to eat or drink anything she concocted. The thought of being poisoned made him shudder. He couldn't wait to get started on the investigation.

If anything's here, it will be uncovered, lady!

EPILOGUE

—◆•◆❖◆•◆—

The spring of 1877 found Frank McGill, the infamous White Comanche, sitting in a barren, isolation cell of the Texas State Prison waiting to be hung by the neck until dead. After seeing a vision of himself choking on one last breath he made the decision to die and be buried as an Irishman. Leading double identities and shifting between two opposing cultures, had taken its toll and finally broken his spirit to pieces. Once living became just a labor to bear, he'd handed himself over to the law. The tiring cat and mouse game he played for so long was finally over.

Stealing an indulgent look at Stone and his little brother, Clay, was his final pleasure above the grass. One boy was the spitting image of a robust, red-headed, McGill Irishman, and the other was the exact opposite. He was leaner in build with dark, thick hair and a light skin tone like Nacona. There was no mistaking whose seed fathered either of these boys. Even a crusted, black heart like Franklin McGill swelled with pride on recognizing his own flesh and blood.

He owed Mary Ann and Greyson Byrd for keeping them safe and raising them well. Someday, Stone and Clay would be respected ranchers in their own rights. Frank felt uncharacteristically sorrowful for not knowing his children, but it was best the secrets of their lineage be kept from them until reaching maturity. Their parents would guard the past until the time was right.

It had been easy to read the regret in the rangers eyes the day he and Marshal JD Stearns took him into custody. The lawman's regret of the fate his sons' own kin would meet was written on his face. Frank's execution was scheduled to be carried out in a few days for his many crimes against society. He was not surprised when the guard informed him of a visitor. He'd expected the ranger would want to talk. Being a decent man, he inquired first if Frank needed anything. Indeed, Frank had an answer ready.

"I'd like to see the boys' mother before I die. It's important, and I want to talk to both of you together. I would appreciate the chance if you'll allow it."

"It doesn't please me to bring Mary Ann to the prison. She knows your sentence and is grieved for the sake of the boys. Being with child again, I dread for her to make the trip to Huntsville, but once, you spared my wife from being violently raped by two other outlaws even if you were only the lesser of two evils, I am eternally grateful. I also am sure Mary Ann wouldn't have made it home after her pa took her if you hadn't helped. JD and I might not have survived either. For saving all our lives, I'm indebted to you and will try to get her here."

Grey cleared his throat and continued. "I came today to thank you for my boys. Stone and Clay are gifts of great value only you could have given me. I'm pleased to have them in my life and claiming them as my own sons is an honor. No one has ever questioned their belonging to Mary Ann or me. You were right to send Stone home with Clay's mother to be raised beside his blood brother. They are both good, kind, smart, wonderful fellows and are very close and loyal to each other.

"Stone is a big, strong, curly-headed fellow with a ruddy complexion. He never knows a stranger and always has a smile on his face along with something funny to say. He's good natured, anxious to do his share, and is happy. He's an astute horseman and already learning and developing his skills. Clay favors you more physically. He's a lanky, handsome kid with light skin and dark brown hair. He's smart, curious about everything, always reading, good with numbers, and keeps track of details. He has a heart for ranching. I can see both boys raising cattle and horses together someday.

"They love Sari, their sister, and are protective of her which she typically finds annoying. There is a little sister named Ava. Mary Ann says it's an old Irish name, and then there's the new baby on the way." Grey smiled.

"I owe you a debt of gratitude, Frank. It's the reason I'm agreeing to bring Mary, and I will do my best to get her here in time to see you alive, but I can't promise. I also want you to know I was truly sorry the day JD and I arrested you. There was no joy in bringing you to trial." Then, Greyson Byrd nodded his head and left.

In two days, Franklin was informed his hanging had been postponed two weeks. He had no doubt Grey had arranged the rescheduling so Mary could come. His unlikely friend, a Texas ranger, was making a great effort on his behalf. A few days later, Franklin had been shackled, cuffed, and led out of his small cell. The guard he respected most led him to a whitewashed, windowless room with a splintery table and three chairs. Grey was standing back, and Mary Ann was seated. The guard led him to the opposite side of the table and secured him to it by a chain. Before he left the room, he pulled two envelopes out of his pocket and put them in front of Frank.

"After the guard left, Grey was the first to speak. "I'm not sure why you needed to see us both, but we're here as requested. Say your peace. We're both sorry we can't do more for you, but we'll listen."

"Based on my squandered life, this may sound incredible, but my father was a respected banker holding legitimate interests in numerous business ventures. Most everything he touched profited. By the time of his death, he was a relatively wealthy man. His children were equally named in his will. Even though I was estranged from him, he didn't discriminate against me. I have two brothers who followed in his footsteps and agreed to manage my share along with their shares. The money and holdings grew and have been divided among the three of us. My portion is in The First Street Bank of San Antonio which they jointly own. In this envelope is a document naming Stone and Clay Byrd the legal owners of the money. When they come of age, it will be released to them on proof of identity and their signatures."

If Grey was surprised, he didn't show it. He made a promise. "I'll see they get it."

"I wish to be buried on your ranch where the boys are being raised. I know it's a lot to ask, but I don't expect to be put in the family cemetery, just in a marked grave on a hill somewhere. I would like for the tombstone to read my name, date of birth, date of death, and Man of Aoife. The information is written in this second envelope. If you don't agree to this, I understand but please have my body buried somewhere else with this marker."

"Mary and I will discuss this, and you can rest assured it will be taken care of one way or the other," Grey said.

Concentrating on Mary Ann, Frank asked, "Cigala, did you ever find out what happened to the man you called your pa?" He glanced at Grey when he asked her this question.

"I hope to never see him again, but no, wherever he is still a mystery. I've always wondered if he'll show up to cause more trouble someday."

"You have no reason to fear him any longer. I know for a fact the man you thought was you father died long before you and the men made it back to the ranch." Frank made a long moment of eye contact with Grey, trying to convey the truth of it.

Mary was disbelievingly confused. "I believe you think he's dead, but I don't understand how you can say he's not my father." Panic had leaked into her voice, and Greyson stepped behind her putting steady, firm hands on her shoulders.

Frank said, "I'm sorry for upsetting you, Cigala, but I thought you should know this man is dead. As to whether you are related to him, your husband can help you find the truth. Thank you for generously coming as I asked. Thank you for listening to me and thank you for standing by the boys."

Frank cleared his throat with a slight choking sound and called for the guard who came in immediately. Greyson helped his wife up and shook Frank's hand in goodbye, though it was clumsy with him being cuffed and the chain rattling. Tears of heartache streamed down Mary Ann's cheeks. She kept her head down and leaned her weight on Grey. She did not look at Nacona again. Soon the room was quiet and empty as if no one had been there.

Texas State Prison in Huntsville

The Brazos Agency served Indians along the main fork of the Brazos River near Fort Belknap in Young County. The Comanche Agency was included and served the Southern Band of Comanches 35 miles southwest of Belknap.

Texas Rangers 1887

Texas Rangers, Company "D" at Realitas, Texas, in 1887. Back row from left: Jim King; Bass Outlaw; Riley Boston; Charles Fusselman; Mr. Durbin; Ernest Rogers; Chas. Barton; Walter Jones; Sitting: Bob Bell; Cal Aten; Capt. Frank Jones; Walter Durbin; Jim Robinson; Frank Schmidt. (Title and photo copyrighted by E.R.Ross.)

The Texas Ranger motto of the day was, "No man in the wrong can stand up against a fellow who's in the right and keeps on a comin'!"

FROM THE AUTHOR

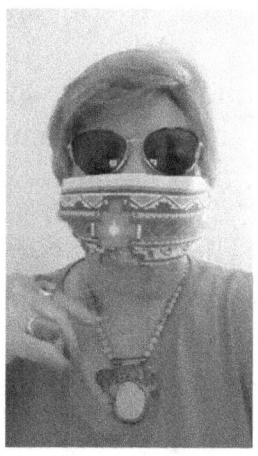

What a year! Who would have thought a pandemic could create such productive isolation? I had plenty of downtime to write and wearing masks and entering places of business in disguise put my imagination in high gear. Scenarios involving outlaws, prairie patrolmen, early ranchers, and the women who loved them bombarded my mind.

My musings whirled with visions of steadfast law dogs fighting evil, hard-working men carving out pieces of the land, criminals pillaging, and indigenous peoples being unfairly displaced to make room for settlers.

The immigrant men wanted to marry and raise families, but on the West Texas prairie of the 1800s white females were scarce. Arranged marriages, mail order brides, and marriages of convenience were practical and commonplace solutions. I like to think the newlyweds found true love. Yes, I'm a dreamer, but in my cowgirl heart, I'm a romantic.

The old west was a fascinating time filled with multifaceted characters, lots of action, heartaches, and victories. The saga of the Bryd Ranch and its courageous people can't be contained in one volume. The story will unfold in three standalone books starting in 1869 with Broken Pieces.

www.ingramcontent.com/pod-product-compliance
Lightning Source LLC
Chambersburg PA
CBHW051432170626
46809CB00006B/2423